Chloe Lane is a writer and the founding editor of Hue+Cry Press. *The Swimmers* is her first novel and was longlisted for the Ockham New Zealand Book Awards 2021. She lives in Christchurch, New Zealand with her husband and young son.

The Swimmers

Chloe Lane

Gallic Books
London

A Gallic Book
First published by Te Herenga Waka University Press
New Zealand in 2020

© Chloe Lane 2020
Chloe Lane has asserted her moral right to be identified
as the author of the work.

First published in Great Britain in 2022 by
Gallic Books, 12 Eccleston Street, London, SW1W 9LT

A CIP record for this book is available from the British Library

ISBN 978-1-913547-31-8

Typeset in Minion Pro by Gallic Books
Printed in the UK by CPI (CR0 4YY)

2 4 6 8 10 9 7 5 3 1

For my family

Contents

The Saturday Before

1

'It's a painting show,' I said. 'Geometric abstraction.'

'Geometric abstraction,' Aunty Wynn said.

'Shapes,' I said. 'Squares and triangles, etcetera.'

I had no desire to discuss art with Aunty Wynn. This was the first time she had shown any interest in my interests. I had my mother to blame for these questions about my recent curatorial debut, and while trapped inside a car.

'I can remember the difference between an isosceles triangle and the other one.' It was typical of Aunty Wynn to veer the conversation into a zone where she could be in control, in the know. 'The isosceles and the triangle with three sides the same.'

'You mean the equilateral,' I said. 'And there's the scalene—you've forgotten that one.'

'I don't know about that,' she said. 'That doesn't ring a bell.'

Then, before I could respond, as if it were the only play she could think of to again shift the subject of attention in her favour, Aunty Wynn tugged hard on the steering wheel, and I was thrown sideways in my seat.

'Shivers,' she said. She brought the car to an uneasy but deliberate stop on the grassy verge on the wrong side of the road. She hadn't lost control of the vehicle—she had seen something. 'Look at that.'

I was holding a brown paper package of raw meat that Aunty Wynn had collected from the butcher shop after collecting me from the bus stop. It was our red meat for the long weekend. She had insisted I nurse the parcel, which was the size of my head,

all the way to the Moore family house. I was no vegetarian, but the car was filled with the stench of uncooked beef and lamb. I'd already spent two hours on the bus. Now I just wanted to reach our destination and see my mother, whom I hadn't seen in nearly a month. I wasn't interested in any kind of delay.

I squinted through the dirty windscreen. 'Look at what?'

Aunty Wynn flung open her door and skidded down the small gravelly ditch, and was climbing over the wire fence that separated the verge from the paddock before I saw, strung up by its horns and swinging from a low branch of a bare pōhutukawa about twenty metres away, the stricken goat. The animal's back hooves were a foot off the ground. I could hear it bleating. It was a wretched sound. The desperation in its cries, now waning, now increasing.

I had no intention of getting involved. I hadn't even planned on coming north for Queen's Birthday weekend. Only a last-minute change of circumstance had dragged me out of my previous obligation at Mean Space, the gallery where I'd been interning the last six months or so, and where I'd just curated my first show. Knowing how much it meant to me to have my foot in the door with Auckland's art scene, my mother would have been the first to be baffled by my affair with Karl, the gallery's director. The affair had ended abruptly on Friday, after Karl's wife found us in the storage room, backed hard against a rack of paintings covered in bubble wrap and corrugated cardboard, our hands down each other's pants. I hadn't told my mother that was why I'd changed my mind about attending the annual Moore family lunch. I hoped she thought it was because I missed her.

I watched Aunty Wynn from the safety of the passenger seat. Her figure was that of a woman who had once been an athlete but who hadn't managed to keep a full grip on her fitness through middle age. She was in her late fifties, older than my mother by a couple of years, and, as of two weeks prior, my

mother's primary caregiver. She was standing with her hands on her hips with her back to me. Her three-quarter-length turquoise pants were made from a synthetic material that clung to her legs and was bunched up around her backside and waist from the time she had been sitting in the car. On her feet were brand new Nikes, road-cone orange. She was a confusion of wealth and small-town fashion sense. The goat was bleating and softly swinging beside her. I guessed she was figuring out how to extract it from the branch without getting kicked or head-butted. As I was reassuring myself that she wouldn't trust me to be of use anyway, she turned and flapped her arm in a way that suggested she expected me to join her. I pretended I couldn't see.

Like I said, I had no intention of getting involved. I was a born and raised city girl—starting in Wellington and recently settling in Auckland. I looked out my side window: roughly sealed road, ditch, wonky wire and wood fence, empty hump of paddock, three dusty nīkau palms. It was a mirror image of the scene out the other window. Except for those exotic-looking nīkau palms, which appeared alien against that gorse-ravaged backdrop.

'Hello, Erin,' Aunty Wynn called.

I turned to witness her putting her fingers in her mouth and whistle at me like she was summoning a sheepdog.

'Erin! This fellow and I are going to need some assistance.'

In what was admittedly a pretty petulant move, I heaved the package in my lap onto the driver's seat, but with too much force so it bounced and rolled out the open door. I could clearly see Aunty Wynn's face as she watched her bundle of sausages and chops reach the centre of the ditch. Next she looked at me with the kind of expression my mother had used all those times when as a teenager I'd come home at three in the morning stinking of rum and Cokes, with mince-and-cheese pie spillage down the front of my outfit.

I collected the meat package on my way to join Aunty Wynn in the paddock.

The goat was bigger up close. Its coat was off-white with a clean brown splotch on its back, and it had a beard that looked as though it had recently been trimmed and conditioned. Its horns were both hooked around and wedged into a fork of the lowest branch of the pōhutukawa. It wasn't clear how it had got stuck that way. Its yellow eyes were round with panic, but beyond that they were just cold animal eyes. I didn't feel comfortable being that close to it.

'We're going to have to lift him up off the branch and this way a bit,' Aunty Wynn said, as if none of this was new to her. 'He'll kick and it might not be pretty, but it's the only way.'

For decades Aunty Wynn had worn large unflattering glasses, similar to those of the Queen, but in the last year she had updated to more modern frames coated in a cheap turquoise that brilliantly matched her pants. They were exactly the kind of glasses you would expect a small-town nurse to wear. From beneath a helmet of curly auburn hair, she blinked at me through her thick lenses, waiting for me to respond.

'How'd it get like this in the first place?' I asked.

The goat was wearing a collar, and attached to the collar was a long metal chain, which trailed back down the paddock towards a triangular hut constructed out of pinewood and rusted-up corrugated iron. I'd seen several of those goat huts already on our drive from the bus stop.

'Goats like to jump about.' Aunty Wynn said this in her most condescending tone. 'Though I've always thought they must have bad depth perception—you wouldn't believe some of the places I've found various goats.'

'Like where?' I asked.

Aunty Wynn shook her head and smiled. I could see her mind turning, remembering those various goats. She had no intention of sharing them with me.

My mother and I had always approached the annual Moore family gathering—which for reasons that had never been revealed were always held on the most innocuous of public holidays, Queen's Birthday Monday—as if it were something to win. Me and Mum against the rest of them. Every exchange was up for grabs. In that moment I hated Aunty Wynn for keeping me out of the loop about her various goat rescues, for the small power she wielded.

'What do you want me to do then?' I said, determined to win something back. I placed the meat package on the grass beside me and clapped my hands.

'I'm going to give this fellow a hug,' Aunty Wynn said. She was wearing a baggy grey-marle sweatshirt with two pink dolphins embroidered over her heart. She rolled up her sleeves to reveal two soft freckled forearms. 'Then I'm going to lift him up and sideways so you can unhook his horns.'

'Yup,' I said, pretending I was bored.

I moved so I was standing directly opposite the goat. Despite the pitched angle of its head, and the branch between us, I could see into both its eyes. I wondered whether it knew we were trying to help. It hadn't made any move to kick. In fact, if it weren't for its fraught bleats, I would have said it seemed weirdly resigned to its hanging position in that tree.

Now Aunty Wynn leaned in, and with a 'Here I go' she grabbed the goat around its middle. That started it kicking—Aunty Wynn was only just out of reach of its hooves. Its four legs went wild. It was running for its life.

'I'm going to lift him on the count of three,' she said.

She counted down and then she raised the goat up with a groan, lifting it clear of the branch, after which I managed to unhook the horns so she was free to set it down and jump out of its way. Once the goat's hooves hit the earth it bolted away from us with such force and speed that it nearly decapitated itself when the chain connecting its collar to its hut snapped

taut. It fell to the ground in a heap and let out a high bleat.

'He'll be fine,' Aunty Wynn said matter-of-factly.

The whole scene happened very quickly. I was bowled over by the thrill of it. My heart was racing. I watched the goat for a moment, lying on its side, panting, silent, and then I turned to Aunty Wynn. I was beaming.

I swam three kilometres most days. In the last year and a bit, since my mother had been diagnosed with motor neurone disease, I hadn't missed more than one day a week. In my peak racing years, I'd swum more, much more. I'd won national-level medals. But the strength I felt in the pool had never really flowed over into other parts of my life. Aunty Wynn's physical strength wasn't surprising—she'd had a more successful swimming career than I. It was her self-assuredness that impressed me. I couldn't think of anything I'd done recently with equal conviction. For the first time in twenty-six years of annual Moore family lunches and one funeral—those were the only times we ever saw each other—I caught myself, if not admiring, then envying her.

'That was pretty cool,' I said. It was the most positive thing I'd ever said to Aunty Wynn.

She pushed at the sleeves of her sweater again so they were up over her elbows. She wasn't smiling—she was staring into the distance, her mouth moving ever so slightly, as if she were doing sums in her head.

'Should we check the goat's okay?' I asked.

Behind her: a monotone grey sky, more gorse-riddled paddocks, a few mānuka trees huddled together in a lonely group. I thought I could smell the sea, though I couldn't see or hear it.

'I wanted to tell you about a man I saw on TV,' Aunty Wynn said, ignoring my question about the goat's state of health. 'His wife had MND and he was talking about how his wife didn't

die when they thought she would. She kept on. But only after she could do nothing but move her eyes.' She said this quickly, rushing to get it out.

When my mother was diagnosed with motor neurone disease in February the previous year, I'd binged on all the information I could find about it. I was surprised and annoyed to learn that Aunty Wynn—the nurse!—hadn't done the same.

'It's called locked-in syndrome,' I said.

Aunty Wynn nodded as if this wasn't actually new information. 'The wife would watch him as he walked around the room,' she said. 'He said he'd be vacuuming her bedroom, and her eyes would follow him back and forth across the end of the bed.' She sucked her top teeth against her bottom lip, then inhaled sharply and looked directly at me. 'Are you worried this will happen to your mum?'

I knew there was a small chance my mother's decline might plateau right before death. It had been some time since she had been able to speak. She could no longer eat or drink— all nutrients arriving through a plastic tube on a direct route through her stomach wall. And she could only move about on her own with the aid of a four-wheeled walker. With her doctor's shaky prognosis, and a law of averages guiding us, we were prepared for her to continue this downhill slide for another two or three months. Yet the idea that her decline, however painful and hideous, might slow, that she might remain in this current state, or worse, for an unknowable amount of time— that seemed like the sort of next-level tragedy that would befall someone else. But I didn't know how to admit that. Or if I even should.

'No, you don't need to answer that question,' Aunty Wynn said, as if reading my mind.

The goat was standing up now, a few metres away. It looked calmly in our direction and then slowly lowered its head

and enjoyed a large mouthful of thistle. It appeared to have gotten over its recent trauma. I, too, had already forgotten the excitement.

'She's been feeling funny lately,' Aunty Wynn said, though this comment felt like the tail end of a much longer statement. She had been having an internal dialogue with herself, and now she needed to share part of it with me. 'She's been good, really good, but also.'

'Good?' I said. I was picking at the bark of the low-hanging branch of the pōhutukawa—it was soft after recent rain. I'd already picked away a scab the size of my fist. 'But she can't do any of the things she loves to do. She can't go anywhere on her own. She can't eat, she can't drink her gin and tonics. She barely has enough energy to read. Her life has gotten shittier and shittier.'

'Yes,' Aunty Wynn said. 'She's good though. You'll see.'

'Good?' I said, my voice a register higher this time. I didn't believe it. I threw another chunk of bark back at the tree.

Now Aunty Wynn was rolling her shoulders so her arms danced loose at her side. I recognised the action—she was a swimmer loosening up before a race. It was something I used to do. Then she briefly closed her eyes, and for a second her face appeared almost regal. 'She's good,' she said again, taking a deep breath and exhaling audibly through her nose. 'Though you should know, your mum has asked me to help her exit.'

'Exit?' I said.

'Die,' Aunty Wynn said.

She was incredible to watch, my mother had once said about Aunty Wynn. She was talking about when they were both young and still swimming competitively. *Despite how she holds herself on land these days, back then she moved through the water as effortlessly as a goddamn dolphin.* It was, to my knowledge, the only nice thing my mother had ever said about her sister. I remembered this as proof that my mother wouldn't enlist

Aunty Wynn in this way. The idea of my mother checking out made no sense. And even if it could be true, she would have asked me first.

'The law doesn't agree with us, Erin.' Aunty Wynn reached for the package of meat, which was still lying on the grass near my feet. She scooped it up with one hand and lodged it in her armpit. 'We both thought you had a right to know.' Her cheeks and neck had flushed a blotchy crimson. She looked deeply unhappy.

'I don't believe you,' I said.

Just then the goat let out a horrific cry. It startled us both. In the time we'd been talking, the goat had planted itself on the top of its corrugated-iron hut. I hadn't even noticed it walking back down the paddock, let alone scaling the side of its house. Its cry was victorious. I had a vision of firing a bullet clean through the side of its skull.

'Mum hasn't said anything about this to me,' I said. I'd never fired a gun, but in that moment I felt certain I could. In the same way I felt certain that Aunty Wynn had no idea what she was talking about.

Aunty Wynn moved towards me, and I realised she was coming in for a hug. I stepped away. I could think of nothing more repulsive.

'I don't believe you,' I said again. I was beginning to feel the cold, and shivered. It was June, and the air felt chilled with the recent rain.

I could tell Aunty Wynn wanted to say something else. She looked at me with fear and embarrassment, and whatever small admiration I'd had for her earlier vanished. She had never appeared so large and imposing, but those pants, that sweater, the way she squinted at me through her terrible turquoise frames—I knew there was no way my mother would give herself up to that woman. It was like a strange Mexican standoff, the two of us unmoving beside the single pōhutukawa, the goat

refereeing from the roof of its hut, but no other witnesses coming or going along the winding road. I'd never felt so alone.

'Let's get this meat home and into the fridge,' Aunty Wynn said finally. And that was all she said before she sadly marched her way back down the paddock.

I had no choice but to follow.

2

I once made an infographic for high school art history that included all of the major advancements in twentieth-century abstraction, beginning with Gauguin and ending with the Abstract Expressionists. Picture a metre-wide cardboard construction, complete with pale, stripy ink-jet examples of works from each period. Recently, I was having days when I thought about the time since my mother had been diagnosed, and I could hold it in my mind as one unbroken line—the decline of her health becoming its own kind of infographic. And sometimes I visualised each step in her decline as parallel to a significant art historical plot point: my mother tripping on the carpet for the second time in a week (Cézanne's Mont Sainte-Victoire), beginning to slur her words (Sonia Delaunay's 'Prismes électriques'), losing control of her hands (a Mondrian *composition*), losing control of her bowels (Rothko).

I doubted it was healthy for me to do this. I hadn't read any books on grief, or sought counselling, and I rarely spoke to my friends about my mother's illness. They knew—I just didn't talk about it. I couldn't imagine my life without my mother in it—of course I couldn't—and I felt like shit all of the time, but *weird* was often the word that rolled through my mind. When people asked how my mother was doing, more than once I'd responded with a cool overview, followed by, 'Yeah, it's pretty weird.'

Standing in the Moore family kitchen for only the second time in my life, I had that same inane thought: this is just weird. I also felt calm. The dead calm of a deep, dark lake,

where things brush against your legs while you're swimming.

My mother and I had always hosted the annual family lunch, so the only other time I'd visited the Moore family house, even though I now lived only two hours south, was sixteen years earlier, when my grandfather died. Aunty Wynn had lived in this house her whole life with the oldest Moore sibling, my Uncle Cliff, and though the farm hadn't functioned as a farm in years, the house—a wide bungalow in desperate need of a paint job, with its waist-high wire fence rimming the yard— was exactly as I remembered it. Except now it stood on the edge of a subdivision of sprawling brick-and-tile kitset homes, all with stunted flax bushes and bare hydrangea shrubs lining the driveways.

I'd come prepared to stay two nights. It was the most I could swing away from my thesis, and paid and unpaid work. My mother knew that. From the beginning, she had insisted life should go on as normal. 'I don't want you moping around the place any more than usual,' she had said, many times. Since then I'd flown home to Wellington about once every month, give or take, which was about twice as often as before.

My satchel on one shoulder, my overnight bag on the other, and still clutching the large parcel of uncooked meat, I stared out the window and into the backyard of one of those new kitset houses, where two small children were jumping on a trampoline. *Gleeful* is the word I would use to describe them. My great-grandmother had once looked through this same window when the farm had stretched all the way to the black-sand mudflats of the Kaipara Harbour and the hills beyond.

Some might consider that landscape beautiful. Rita Angus, the primary artist I was writing about for my master's, sure did. Though she hadn't studied these exact hills, she had painted others like them, and relentlessly—paintings that had already been written about relentlessly too. For that reason alone, she

wasn't an original topic choice—something which pained me to admit.

The trampoline had a high soft fence around it. The children, who wore gumboots and ankle-length yellow anoraks, stopped jumping and the girl knotted the sleeves of the boy's anorak at his back like handcuffs. When the girl resumed jumping, the boy lost his balance and instantly fell to his knees, bouncing head first against the trampoline's protective fence before falling face first against his sister's boot. The girl froze and looked in the direction of the house as the boy began to howl. No one rushed outside.

Hearing that boy's cries made me painfully aware of the deep silence in the house behind me and how nervous I was about seeing my mother. She had stopped being able to talk before my last visit, before she left our Wellington home and moved here and into Aunty Wynn's care.

'Is your tummy better?' Aunty Wynn said in her best nurse's voice. She had appeared in the kitchen hugging a sack of potatoes: our vegetable for the long weekend.

'It's perfect,' I said, though it wasn't completely true. After five silent minutes back on the road, I'd thrown up—on the dashboard, car seat and floor, though not on my shoes. I wasn't used to country roads. Aunty Wynn wasn't upset—she handled the mess cheerfully, which only made me feel more humiliated. Now I placed the parcel of meat on the kitchen counter while I observed Aunty Wynn staring at my waist, my legs, my waist again.

'I meant to say earlier, you're all skin and bones,' she said. The sack of potatoes was slipping and she adjusted her grip.

I looked down at my T-shirt and cardigan, my old blue jeans. They were all loose. It was true I'd lost a lot of weight in the last twelve months. The second-to-last time I'd seen Karl the gallery director, one of only three times we'd got ourselves a bed instead

of a dusty storage room, he had snatched at my bare thighs, my ankles hooked over his shoulders, and whispered, not to me but to himself, like a scientist making a field recording: 'Lovely lean drumsticks.' If I hadn't fallen so hard and fast for him, I might have been able to admit how much it had repulsed, even alarmed, me.

While a couple of my oldest friends had expressed concern about my health, most were quick to say how good I looked, which meant they were impressed with how thin I'd become. The compliments made me feel like I was handling it, like I was on top of it all. Though whenever I see photos of myself from this time, I think of the expression 'bright-eyed and bushy-tailed' and how much I looked the opposite. Not tired or sick, exactly, not really even too thin. More like I'd been through the wash too many times. Faded out. Less *there*.

Aunty Wynn took a couple of wide steps towards me and dropped the sack of potatoes on the floor. She lingered, and for a moment it seemed like she didn't quite know what to do with her face. 'She'll be awake,' she said. Then she stretched up tall, planted her hands on her hips and confidently beamed at me: the woman of the house.

Looking at her standing like that made me newly grateful to my mother for being the one Moore sibling who had managed to get away. And then, in a heartbeat, I remembered that now, nearly forty years later, she'd had to move back.

Carrying my bags, I trailed Aunty Wynn out of the kitchen and into the hallway, following the bottom stroke of the hallway's backwards L shape. When I entered the small room to the left I was struck by the shelves crammed with hundreds of dolphins of varying sizes and colours and made out of wood, ceramic, glass, crystal, plastic, shells, and were those pine cones? The curtains had been drawn so the only decent light was a low-watt ceiling bulb and the faint glow of my mother's iPad, as she sat diminished and propped up in a loaned hospital bed. To

her right there was a metal frame, which her feeding bag come mealtime could be suspended from. The dolphins didn't cheer things up.

'Here she is,' Aunty Wynn said commandingly from the end of the bed.

As I emerged from behind Aunty Wynn, my mother let out a shrivelled-up cry. I could tell she was laughing but the sound she made wasn't my mother's laugh. It frightened me.

'Doesn't she look good?' Aunty Wynn said.

I'd expected her to look worse somehow. I think I'd expected Aunty Wynn to have her dressed in some kind of old lady's nightgown, maybe an off-white flannel with tiny pale pink flowers on it. Instead, my mother was wearing a loud seventies-style yellow and green frock with capped sleeves. I'd never seen that frock before. I couldn't remember the last time my mother had worn a frock for any occasion. A string of large yellow beads hung around her neck.

My mother was pointing at her hair and nodding at me. I'd dyed my hair a few days before and, while the box had described the dye as 'darkest intense auburn', the result was more of a pink grapefruit. When I emailed my mother a photo she had responded: OH NO MY DAUGHTER HAS JOINED A CULT WHERE THEY WEAR WATERMELON HATS. Her comment didn't really make sense, but it had deflated me. She could still be blunt—her illness hadn't changed her that much.

Mere minutes before he dumped me, Karl had said—his voice dry with lust, his lips brushing my neck—that I looked like the girl from *The Fifth Element*. Remembering this now, a confused shiver of pleasure and anxiety zipped along my spine. I combed at my hair with my fingers. 'It looks dumb, doesn't it?'

My mother leaned back into her pillow and shook her head weakly. She did look frailer than she had the last time I'd seen her.

'Your hair?' Aunty Wynn said to me. Then turning back to my mother: 'It's very bold, isn't it, Helen?'

My mother didn't respond, which was exactly how I expected her to treat her sister. She had given her that cold shoulder my whole life. I felt secure knowing that much hadn't changed, that my mother and I were still allies. I placed my bags on the floor and sat on the edge of her bed. The high metal frame creaked. With one weak hand she turned her iPad towards me. This was how she communicated all the time now—the screen full of giant uppercase text.

SOS I CAN'T SPEND ANOTHER MOMENT WITH THESE FUCKING DOLPHINS

I knew how long it would have taken my mother to type that message. She used Word because she didn't like the text programmes that were 'too pushy with their corrections'. I pictured her hands gliding slowly and awkwardly over the screen, woodpecking out each letter, deleting the unintentional typos, the slipping of her fingers, typing it again. I loved that this was the most urgent thing she wanted to share with me in that moment, and it meant even more because of the effort involved.

I glanced at Aunty Wynn, who was still hovering at the end of the bed, the shelves behind her crammed with ugly dolphins. She pushed the bridge of her glasses up her nose with one soft index finger and smiled, as if she were in on the joke. 'I'll leave you ladies to catch up,' she said. Then she left the room.

'Do you want me to smash them?' I asked jokingly, holding fast to the knowledge that my mother and I were a team.

She attempted a smile. When I sat this close to her, the difficulty with which she moved her limbs, the fact she could no longer talk, and the slackness of her face all faded into the periphery, and I saw that my whole hilarious and sharp-tongued mother was still there. There was no glazing over

of her eyes. She held my gaze the same way she had for the previous twenty-six years of my life: confidently, questioning, and ready to laugh. I hadn't realised how much I'd missed her.

But something had changed since I'd seen her last.

When she was eighteen my mother had gone to university in Wellington, then lived in London for a stint before returning to Wellington where she had worked at the National Library since the early nineties, after I was born. Her life didn't seem that remarkable to me, but she had told me more than once that the reason she had never been close to her brother and sister was because they had never forgiven her for moving so far away—for having a life that was different from theirs. When I'd asked what had stopped Aunty Wynn and Uncle Cliff from leaving the family farm, my mother simply said, 'Your grandfather couldn't hack looking after the farm on his own. I only got to leave because he liked me least.'

In my opinion, my mother had got the better deal, but that bitterness had followed her around her entire life. I'd rarely heard her mention her family or speak to them without sharpness in her voice (her admiration for Aunty Wynn's athleticism was one of those rare moments). Even if it was difficult to gauge the tone of her written words, her quip about Aunty Wynn's dolphins was different, and Aunty Wynn's response confirmed the whole thing as playful. It was impossible to deny that my mother was enjoying herself. I'd never seen her and Aunty Wynn interact like that.

There was something else. I'd dyed my mother's hair during my last visit home. Expecting to see the grey roots showing at her part, I'd bought a box of dye from the pharmacy on my way to the bus stop that afternoon. She wouldn't need me to fix her up, though—her hair had recently been dyed and cut. It was a rich red brown. It was glistening. And she had highlights! I began wondering what kind of drug cocktail Aunty Wynn

might have her on, which led me to my next thought: my mother's decision about wanting to end her life couldn't possibly have been a sober one.

Now she opened another saved note on her iPad. She had obviously prepared a number of things she wanted to say without the pain of typing each letter in front of me.

PLEASE SEND PHOTOS

'I will,' I said.

She meant the photos of the show I'd curated at Mean Space. The internship with Karl was mostly writing emails, visiting the post office, buying coffees and helping to pour drinks at exhibition openings, but a couple of years earlier Karl had started giving his interns the chance to curate their own small group show. It was an exciting opportunity, for sure, but it was also good for him—he could scope out potential new talent without having to lift a finger. My show had opened a couple of weeks ago, and I felt that the reception had been overwhelmingly mediocre. I didn't want my mother to know about the medium-sized turnout at the opening, where people only stayed long enough to drink the free booze, and then the radio silence that followed—no response being much worse than even a scathing review.

'I'll send them to you later,' I said.

My mother was already looking for another pre-prepared note. I scanned the room while I waited. At the foot of the bed was her old TV, sitting on the same wood veneer and glass unit that it had sat on for a decade in our home. She had moved a few other large possessions with her from Wellington—I'd helped her pack them up during my last visit—though the TV was all I recognised. On the bedside table were chunky paperbacks. There were several by Agatha Christie, P. D. James, Ngaio Marsh, as well as a Stephen King and a Dan Brown. Thrillers and whodunits were my mother's reading material

of choice since the disease had slowed her down. 'Dan knows how to keep a reader hooked,' she'd said when I asked why she was reading one of the *Da Vinci Code* books. 'Everyone in my MND group's reading this stuff. We love it. I can fall asleep after ten pages, then when I wake up, I'm straight back into heart-pumping action.' At the bottom of the book pile was a much slimmer volume. It looked out of place beneath those heavy page-turners, but my mother had found what she was looking for.

This new note had the same large text as the previous two, but it disappeared well below the bottom of the screen. It pained me to think about how long it would have taken my mother to type it all. I braced myself: this joking around about Aunty Wynn's dolphins hadn't distracted me from what we most needed to discuss. She nudged the iPad with her hand, and then closed her eyes.

I WAS THINKING ABOUT LAST QUEEN'S BIRTHDAY

It wasn't surprising that even in her current state, and given the difficulty with which she typed, she had abbreviated nothing. She despised text-message speech. This was another reason she liked to write these things in advance—so she had time to get it right.

I GET BORED LYING HERE CORNERED BY MY THOUGHTS. THOUGH WYNN HAS BEEN A HOOT

'Really, a hoot?'

She opened her eyes. Though she could manage few convincing facial movements there was an undeniable secretiveness to her expression. She had never once referred to her sister as a hoot. She usually preferred 'my sister', 'your aunty', 'that woman', 'the Boiled Chicken Queen'. She rarely even referred to her by her first name.

REMEMBER THE FENNEL SALAD YOU MADE. I DIDN'T SAY HOW BAD IT WAS BECAUSE YOU WERE TRYING HARD TO

BRANCH OUT IN THE KITCHEN. IF YOU'RE STILL MAKING IT, CHECK YOU'RE USING RIGHT AMOUNT OF FENNEL FROM BEST PART OF BULB. IT'S AN INTENSE VEGE

When I looked up, my mother was watching me with a small smile.

'Mum?' I said. I'd been expecting to read something completely different. Was she kidding? Had she really spent however long—ten minutes, twenty minutes, maybe longer—typing a warning about my fennel salad?

Her joyful expression faltered. She looked tired. I had the horrible realisation that I was the source of her present tiredness—my response had disappointed her. She wanted to keep things light and I'd failed to play along. Before I could say anything else she opened another of her notes.

WYNN TOLD YOU I WANT TO GET THIS THING OVER WITH. I'M SORRY I COULDN'T TELL YOU. THIS TYPING BULLSHIT DIDN'T SEEM LIKE THE RIGHT WAY

We looked hard at each other then. My mother had rusty swamp-coloured eyes. I'd always been glad I'd gotten my father's pale blues, not her muddy specimens, and I had this same silly thought again now.

'When?' I managed, my voice ripe with adrenalin.

I wanted to look elsewhere as she typed. The disease had started in her hands and her feet. There was that week she had tripped on the hall carpet twice. Then she had dropped a stack of dinner plates while unloading the dishwasher. She had said that had frightened her most, watching her hands give out like that. Like the bottom falling out of a paper shopping bag—all the strength in them just *gone*. Now it was hard to watch her clawed hands move slowly and shakily over the screen, but I did watch; I watched as she typed out each painful letter. It was the best I could offer her in that moment.

She turned the screen to face me.

TUESDY

I felt something heavy hit the floor of my chest. My mother was watching me with eyes round with relief. She raised a thin shaky arm and placed her hand gently against my cheek. It was such a small gesture, but she had never cradled my face like that. It wasn't how we did things. We were not the kind of family who hugged, who told each other *I love you*—the sensation of her hand on my cheek made me feel scared in a new way.

That abbreviation—or was it a typo?—was out of character for my mother too. 'This Tuesday?' I said. Then, 'Why?'

Behind the note where she had typed that single word, I could see the top of her long, silly bit about my fennel salad. I felt certain that her decision about the end of her life would have preceded her typing of that warning. The thought of her quietly chuckling over each of those pecked-out words, when the countdown on her life had already begun, was one thing—mortifying, yes—but that she didn't get the result she had hoped for—a laugh from her daughter, the one person she could always count on for a laugh—made it even more miserable. I felt strangled with guilt. I would have to do better.

A few letters into her response, my mother pressed her finger to the delete key and held it there. She shook her head.

'But it's so soon,' I said. I wanted to know what had happened, what had changed in the two weeks since she had moved into Aunty Wynn's care. I eyed the shelves of dolphin ornaments and thought, This is my fault. Because I had not found a way to take care of her in her own home, she was giving up. I'd made this happen. And then I thought: But what about me? Why would she want to leave me?

My mother was watching me, and waiting. I think she did want to explain. I think she did want to tell me—about each tough new milestone, every new marker on the rocky downhill slalom that had brought her closer to this decision and conversation with her only child, about her fear of no longer

being herself. At the same time, she didn't want to tell me. She didn't want to have to justify what she wanted. That was my mother. She wanted me to accept what she had decided and get on with it.

Tuesday.

'Are you sure?'

She returned a small nod. And just like that, I accepted her choice. Was it the look in her eye that convinced me, or the way she defiantly raised her chin and closed her eyes, her hands folded peacefully one on top of the other like an already-corpse? All of the above and none of the above. I just knew.

My next question was 'How?' but I wasn't ready to hear the answer, so instead I said, 'Of course I'll stay till then.' My hands were trembling. I felt a whirlpool of worry forming in my gut. I looked at the overnight bag sitting on the floor by my feet. 'I haven't brought enough clothes.'

Inside my bag were two pairs of underwear, one bra, two T-shirts, a long-sleeved shirt, and my swimming gear. I hadn't even bothered to pack pyjamas. In a plastic ziplock bag was my toothbrush and a bottle of face moisturiser. How carelessly and sparsely I'd packed for this weekend.

I scanned my mother's face. She looked happier than I thought she should. My eyes fell again to the yellow and green frock she was wearing. It fitted neatly across her broad shoulders, her wasted chest and arms. I realised something then that I should have figured out earlier: this was a dress she used to wear when she was younger, much younger, maybe when she was last living in this house. Then I had another thought: she wants to die in that dress.

I moved mechanically along the dark, narrow hallway and back towards the kitchen. Black-and-white photographs of people I didn't recognise hung above shelves of hardbound and uncracked books from Reader's Digest: Sherlock Holmes, gardening encyclopaedias, a how-to of home medicine. The house had the feel of being both too lived in and entirely free of human attention. There was a rank citrus smell in the air—it could have been from cleaning products or a mandarin that had rolled into a damp corner and was at peak rot. That smell faded into burnt butter and animal fat—Aunty Wynn was frying sausages for dinner. Uncle Cliff was sitting motionless at the kitchen table, an electric heater wheeled up beside him. That bright, dusty corner of the house, with its curling cream and blue vinyl flooring, faded mid-century wallpaper of stone fruits and childish squiggles, the wooden table with four mustard-coloured vinyl chairs, and Aunty Wynn and Uncle Cliff so healthy and present, now infuriated me.

I stood on the threshold between the hallway and kitchen, and a deep shiver ran up my spine and across my shoulders. I twitched wildly, like someone preparing to throw themselves into deep water in the middle of winter. I couldn't help but feel I was no longer walking around on dry land. Other elements were taking charge.

Tuesday.

I yanked out a chair—the legs scraped across the floor with a wretched sound—and parked myself beside Uncle Cliff. He was hunched over a can of Speight's. I wanted to smack him across

the back of the head and wrench him into an upright sitting position. What gave him the right to look so despondent?

'And how're you doing there?' he said, very softly, eyes rising to meet mine, looking every bit his weathered sixty-plus years. He was wearing navy rugby shorts and a pastel yellow polo shirt buttoned to the top. A pair of half-moon glasses hung on a fluorescent yellow cord around his neck. There was such a gentleness about him—I'd forgotten that.

'Honestly?' I said. Though I had no energy or enthusiasm for niceties, I was surprised by how angry I sounded.

Aunty Wynn still had her back to us. 'I'm going to my aqua aerobics class after dinner,' she said, as the enormous chrome fridge in the corner of the room, one of those fancy two-door ones with an ice dispenser on the front, started groaning noisily. 'You want mashed potatoes with your bangers?' She had to speak up to be heard.

'Why not,' I said. I could feel my heart beating in my throat. I was sweating around my hairline, and above my top lip—a nervous sweat made worse by the strength of the nearby heater.

'You can visit Bethany after dinner if you like,' Aunty Wynn said. Bethany was Aunty Wynn's sixteen-year-old daughter whom I hadn't seen since last year's Queen's Birthday lunch. She was of no interest to me—anytime, really, but especially not now. 'She's living in one of the houses we snapped up in the subdivision across the paddock. Though she's at school till the end of next year, we decided to give her more leash to run with.'

Aunty Wynn had convinced my mother to cash out her share of the farm when my grandfather died. My mother had wanted to give it up, but within a couple of years Aunty Wynn and Uncle Cliff were dividing it up and selling it off for a killing. My mother's payout meant I'd been able to attend a private girls' school in Wellington and I hadn't needed to get a student loan to cover my undergraduate degree, but my aunty and

uncle were sitting pretty now. For years, the only thing they had spent money on were their annual excursions to the Gold Coast and that noisy chrome fridge. So it hadn't surprised my mother and me to learn they had reinvested the money in two kitset houses that had since been built on the original Moore land. They weren't imaginative people.

'Bethany's such a good girl,' Aunty Wynn said. 'Did I tell you she's going to be a vet?' She had turned to face the room and was holding a pan in one hand and a potato masher in the other. 'She hasn't got into vet school yet, but she's real excited about the idea of working with animals—been volunteering at the local clinic once a fortnight, you know.'

As Aunty Wynn spoke, I felt increasingly agitated and then angry about so many things I couldn't order my thoughts well enough to know what to focus on: my mother wanting to check out, my mother not telling me about her decision to check out, Aunty Wynn thinking she was going to help my mother check out. Tuesday. What was that, three sleeps? This whole time, Uncle Cliff had been cradling his beer and staring at the kitchen table. Now I noticed his eyes shifting side to side as if he was reading a newspaper.

'Uncle Cliff,' I said, wanting him to stop. My voice sounded weird—both hard and fragile, like many crushed shells. 'I'm gonna have one of your beers.'

'Oh my goodness, of course,' he said. He jumped up, almost ran to the fridge. Once he handed me the can he sat back down and immediately recommenced staring at the tabletop.

I waited for someone to mention my mother.

'I go to aqua aerobics with one of the new nurses,' Aunty Wynn said. 'A lovely young Samoan girl. She and her husband bought a four-bedroom two doors down from Bethany's place. I guess they're planning on having kiddies.'

No one was going to mention my mother.

How did Aunty Wynn get so much joy from thinking about

another woman's real estate and impending litter of children? How was it she could think about anything else at all? I took a deep gulping swig of beer, not stopping till my eyes started watering. It made me feel better and then much worse. When I finished that beer, I stood and walked to the fridge and helped myself to another. On sitting back down at the table I noticed a small haystack of mustard vinyl on the floor beneath where I'd been sitting—I'd absentmindedly clawed off and shredded a two-centimetre-diameter offering from my chair.

'Their kitchen counter looks like it's made out of real marble,' Aunty Wynn said. 'Sounds pretty swish, doesn't it?'

Just then the fridge's ice dispenser whirred into action and spat out several cubes of ice. They skidded across the floor and under the table. Neither Aunty Wynn nor Uncle Cliff said anything or even seemed to notice. This whole scene in the kitchen—Aunty Wynn with her mindless chatter, Uncle Cliff with his staring—was too much.

Finally I snapped. 'What's wrong with that machine?'

'What's that?' Aunty Wynn said.

'Didn't you see that?' Both Aunty Wynn and Uncle Cliff stared at me. 'The ice machine. It just spewed out a bunch of ice.'

'Don't let it upset you,' Aunty Wynn said. She gently placed my dinner in front of me: a plate set with two sausages, a little hill of mashed potatoes, and a swamp of peas. 'It's just a bit temperamental,' she said, in nearly a whisper, which was unnerving in its own way. She lightly placed her hand on my shoulder—almost a pat, not quite.

The arrangement on my plate was like something out of a postwar commercial for the New Zealand Beef and Lamb Board. The dinner plate was the same Crown Lynn with the faded floral and leaf pattern that my mother and I had had in our Wellington home. The sight of it made me feel less angry and, instead, mortifyingly sad.

'Don't let it upset me,' I said.

Aunty Wynn turned back to the kitchen counter and leaned her weight against the chipped Formica edge—her large hands and wide soft arms two arched flying buttresses. A heavy quiet settled on the room. Uncle Cliff stared at his beer can.

The Kaipara Moores. Simple farming folk. How was it they believed they could master and execute a plan to end the life of one of their own? My mother. Her life! It was almost comical. And, no, I hadn't considered myself part of this group of masterminds, whatever their plan. Though, in my state of sweaty swinging anger and disbelief, I understood enough to know that it was good I was there. A planned, peaceful death was what my mother wanted, and I would have to make sure these morons didn't screw it up.

Uncle Cliff was the one to break the silence.

'That contraption bothers me too,' he said, his eyes narrowed. 'The other day'—he shook his head—'I almost nearly brained myself on a stray ice cube.'

Since I'd learned of my mother's illness, I'd been in a kind of holding pattern—a lone aircraft circling round and round above it all. I think now that I received that small fridge-related confession from Uncle Cliff as a kind of signal, a faint blinking light. It wasn't necessarily one that would allow me to land, but it made me feel less alone up there. It made me feel a little less angry anyway, a little less afraid.

My mother wasn't in her room.

'Mum?' I called. She couldn't call back—I hadn't forgotten—but, as I'd hoped, a *rap rap rap* came from the other end of the L-shaped hallway, near the front of the house.

I ventured back towards the kitchen—empty now, Aunty Wynn and Uncle Cliff having both scarpered after dinner, though Aunty Wynn would be back before eight to discuss 'all the angles' of my mother's death—and then I turned and walked halfway up the vertical stroke of the L before entering the formal dining room. No lights were on in that room but this is what I could see: a polished dark wood table, oval, with crochet cotton runner; six polished dark wood chairs, identical except one; a polished dark wood sideboard, with one near-full bottle of Johnnie Walker and four upside-down crystal glasses; one painting, framed in dark wood, of a scene composed of cows, a stream, hills thick with trees and strangled by clouds.

Individually these objects were unremarkable. But arranged in this unlit, window-free room they looked like a 'How we used to live' scene from the Auckland Museum. All that was missing were a couple of blank-faced mannequins dressed in period-appropriate garb.

Four more impatient raps echoed from the adjacent living room.

It was much brighter in there. The walls were hung with more animal-themed pictures: a square print of roosters and hens in a dusty farmyard, a child's black pen sketch of a dead-eyed rabbit, a cross-stitch of a flat blue dolphin leaping through the

phrase *When life gives you trouble blow bubbles.* To my right was my mother. 'Here you are,' I said.

She had been changed out of her frock and into a soft blue cotton nightie, over which she was wearing a very bright and highly embroidered red, gold and black kimono, the same yellow beads from earlier were hanging around her neck, and there was a pair of cheap leopard-print slippers on her feet. She was sitting in a huge black leather La-Z-Boy chair near an old electric heater. The flat-screen TV in front of her was switched off—the rapping sound had been her whacking the TV remote on the lacquered walnut-textured compartment hidden beneath her right armrest, now exposed. With a crash she dropped the remote back in its place. Her iPad was resting in her lap. She watched me, waiting for me to say something more.

Her walker and feeding paraphernalia had been wheeled in with her too. She had started having difficulty swallowing two months earlier, which was when she'd had the feeding tube put in. My mother had always loved food and drink. She'd had a gin and tonic every evening for the last decade, from around the time I was sixteen and old enough (in her mind) to have a drink with her. She wouldn't be able to do that ever again. I hated that loaned wheelie contraption, its metal frame a dulled stainless steel that suggested too many other slow deaths. When I locked on to it now, and my gaze crept along the tube leading from the suspended plastic pouch of opaque formula—a pale fleshy colour that reminded me of no food—and directly into my mother's stomach, I felt as if something cold and metallic was surging through my bone marrow.

I looked away from where the tube emerged from between the fold of her kimono. 'You're sitting in a La-Z-Boy,' I said.

She had her feet up on the footrest, the body of the chair at a mild tilt so she looked about as comfortable as was humanly possible while also remaining upright enough to safely receive

her dinner. She looked more at ease than I'd seen her in a long time. Her La-Z-Boy was lined up with two others: a brown leather one in desperate need of some moisture, and a plush yet balding blood-red number.

'And there's a fleet of them,' I said.

There are some things one can never be prepared for. Seeing my mother being swallowed by a large leather La-Z-Boy—a symbol of the life of simple comforts, so a symbol of Aunty Wynn and Uncle Cliff's life, so everything my mother had left behind for a life that was different, better—was one of those things. She seemed to have both perked up and shrunken over the course of her nap and our dinner. It was the weirdest sight—because she looked ridiculous but also because she looked so at peace. I was split between wanting to burst out laughing—my mother! In a La-Z-Boy!—and crumbling in a heap. My mother in a La-Z-Boy.

Before all my races, my coach had given me pep talks. Two thirds were devoted to reaffirming my race plan (how many strokes to wind up, split goals, how far out before I would bring it home, etcetera), while the last third was a mix of cross-stitch-worthy phrases like: 'You've done the pain, now's time for the gain' and (simply) 'No wussing out, got it?' and (often) 'If anyone tries psyching you out in marshalling, tell them to go screw themselves.'

If he had been alive and there to witness what I was going through, he would have said, quite plainly, that I was wussing out. Looking at my mother in that chair, I felt like a wuss. She wanted me to keep it light. She was watching me, trying to figure out what I was trying to figure out. I gave her a lightweight smile.

My mother's reply: a wobbly middle finger.

Ever since her speech had first started to fade, thumbs up and thumbs down had become useful communicating devices. So the middle finger had come out of hiding too. Though it had

become increasingly difficult to pull off, my mother was fond of that old gesture—the spirit of it, the small power it gave her. I'd started using it again too. In fact, it was the last gift I gave Karl on Friday afternoon as I'd left Mean Space.

Now, my mother's middle finger—shaky, with her three other fingers and thumb balled satisfactorily and resting on her thigh—told me my smile had been an okay response.

'Sorry,' I said, shrugging theatrically, finding some momentum. 'I just never thought I'd see the day.'

She had something prepared on her iPad.

I BET IT'S UPSETTING SEEING YOUR COOL MOTHER CONFINED TO A LAZY BOY. QUELLE HORREUR PLEASE DON'T REMEMBER ME THIS WAY

Her eyebrows were arched as best as she could arch them. Her eyes were bright.

'Don't worry,' I said. 'My enduring memory of you will be much cooler than this.'

My enduring memory. I felt as if I'd uttered something really filthy. My face suddenly felt hot. And something, some leftover dinner morsel, caught at the back of my throat. A flake of potato skin or pea skin, maybe. I coughed.

My mother looked unimpressed, her face still capable of a convincing frown. I was supposed to be joking around, to be reassuring her. I wasn't playing the game right. A small panic gripped me. 'Sorry,' I said, and again I coughed.

The worst thing was that this picture of my mother, dying in a mild tilt in her La-Z-Boy, was exactly what I would remember. We both knew it. And her making fun of herself barely concealed how reconciled she seemed to this. Sure, it was only a chair. A chair that was very comfortable for a dying body. An electronically operated chair too—now, her feeding bag emptied, she pushed a button and her mild tilt relaxed deeper with a high whirring sound. But it scared me to see her in that chair and to realise that this might be where she

belonged. Forty years later, a life lived, and now she was home as if nothing had changed, taking her place in the family living room among the Moore fleet.

Also, did that mean that this was where I belonged too?

She had another note to show me. She moved impatiently.

PUT ME IN A YELLOW HEXAGONAL COFFIN THEN YOU CAN ROLL ME DOWNHILL INTO HARBOUR

My mother had explicitly stated, many times, that she wanted to be cremated. This wasn't a change of plan—it was another chance for me to redeem myself.

'Absolutely,' I said. 'Roll you like a giant wheel of cheese?'

She smiled faintly.

'And should we all dress up like mice?'

Though it was less confident this time, there was another middle finger for my effort. A small win, but I wasn't having any kind of fun.

'Why doesn't Aunty Wynn get you Netflix or something?' I asked.

The TV hadn't been hooked up to any cable or streaming device, and only two channels were a viewable quality. Channel 1 was playing some kind of farming show: a man on a quad bike with a border collie on the back following cows down a dirt road, the music in the background a nauseating stringy country song. My mother hadn't wanted to see that show. A thumbs down had indicated this. The Channel 2 Queen's Birthday weekend family movie was something I hadn't watched since I was a kid—*Bring It On*. For a moment my mother had looked confused, then she had shrugged her approval.

'I could hook up my Netflix account to your iPad,' I said.

She shook her head in frustration—she didn't want that.

'Okay but if you're going to have a fancy new TV, why wouldn't you get access to more shows?' I said this with a tone

that suggested it was something I would take care of in the next few days, that I already had it under control, and that the only person my mother should be disappointed in was Aunty Wynn.

'It's too expensive.' Aunty Wynn had appeared in the doorway between the living room and the hallway. 'That's why.'

She was wearing a tracksuit the exact colour of raw chicken breast. Her hair was wet and combed back from her face in such a way that gave her the slightly threatening look of a crime family matriarch. She had returned from her aqua aerobics class.

'Tonight,' she said, making theatrical pains to change the subject, 'I learned what the largest living animal is.' She parked herself in the plush red La-Z-Boy, and pulled the wooden lever on the side so she was reclining at a similar tilt to my mother. She let out a long sigh of pleasure. On her feet she wore a pair of scuffed and stained shin-high Ugg boots.

I flat out refused to sit in one of those things, so I was sitting on a hard floral two-seater against the wall. I had been lounging happily enough when it was only me and my mother in the room—leaning on the armrest, my legs extended across two pillows—but at Aunty Wynn's arrival I sat up straight, like an attack dog on high alert.

'The biggest animal? The blue whale.' I said this as deadpan as I could muster.

'Organism,' Aunty Wynn added. 'The largest living *organism* on Planet Earth. So, no, Erin, you're not right there.' She squinted sceptically at the TV.

The cheerleaders in the movie were having an over-the-top yelling match. One of them said something unnecessarily cruel. When my mother and I fought we had been the same—melodramatic, loud, occasionally unforgivably vicious. I didn't miss the possibility of that. Besides, she could be just as vicious with her written words. But I missed hearing her voice. It

was good and deep. Gravelly. Though not from smoking, just naturally, like her person.

'It's not what you think,' Aunty Wynn said. She shook her head with excessive solemnity.

I hadn't gotten over the habit of looking in my mother's direction every time Aunty Wynn said or did something unbearable. I still waited on her response. My ears still waited on her voice. But my mother was wearing only her most disinterested expression.

'I don't think anyone's really thinking anything,' I said.

'I'll tell you what it is,' Aunty Wynn said. She had found some new fire and confidence during her aqua aerobics class. 'It's a fungus. In America. It's nearly four kilometres across. Parasitic, but apparently you can eat it.' Her tone brightened. 'Like a portobello mushroom.'

Aunty Wynn's insane democratic approach to conversation, whereby all viable topics had the potential to be equally enthralling and alarming, so that her tone was consistently upbeat and concerned at the same time, made it hard to maintain emotional traction. It was a strange and dangerous power she wielded. During her one-sided rants, I sometimes found myself confused, about what we were meant to be doing or discussing, about how I was really feeling. Not this time.

We were meant to be discussing the logistics of my mother's suicide.

'This conversation is really fucking unhelpful,' I said.

My mother had been typing on her iPad. She looked up at me, alarmed.

'What?' I said.

Aunty Wynn was staring straight ahead at the TV. I could see the muscles of her jaw contracting, relaxing, contracting. It was almost as if a small mammal was trapped inside her cheeks and trying to dig its way out. Then I thought, that was probably what my profile looked like too.

My mother turned her iPad to face Aunty Wynn.

'I don't know what happens when you touch it,' Aunty Wynn replied. Her elbows were resting on the plush red armrests, her jaw relaxed now. 'Probably something terrible!' She laughed with satisfaction.

My mother laughed too—that frightening shrivelled-up cry.

I saw a swarm of fungus pores erupting from that giant mushroom, or whatever it was, like a swarm of asthma-inducing bees. The idea exposed an unexplored corner of the anxiety vault in my chest.

'All I know is what my Samoan friend told me tonight,' Aunty Wynn added, casually, pulling at the lever on her chair so she was sitting upright.

She looked across my mother's reclining figure and caught my eye. She was warmed up now, jacked and limber for the main event. She didn't return my anger—my jaw the only one clenched tight. She glanced at my mother, who was tapping slowly at her screen, before looking at me again.

'All right,' she said with a new gruffness, a bristly melancholy, 'now we need to discuss all the angles of your mother's exit.'

I didn't like that word: *exit.*

It was from the slim book I'd seen that afternoon on my mother's bedside table, and which, after our discussion, Aunty Wynn would insist I read. Our family wasn't religious, but that word wasn't the kind of word that regular folks, not even religious folks, used to talk about death. Were my mother and Aunty Wynn in a cult now? Because it was the kind of word a charismatic leader might use to trick his followers into thinking of their suicide as a necessary step towards a higher purpose—and here's your glass of Kool-Aid, etcetera.

That word didn't make it any easier for me to face what was really about to happen. Up until this point I'd thought about

my mother's death with the accuracy of a small stupid child. I'd accepted it would be like her going to sleep, like a switch being flicked—no more. When I was that same stupid child I'd also believed people were the same consistency all the way through, as if they were made of plasticine. But now here was the fact of it. My mother wasn't able to swallow pills, so a liquid was the obvious choice. And, because she didn't have an IV drip, she would have to insert the liquid (though, I already feared, with a lot of difficulty) into her feeding tube on her own. There was something additionally disturbing about the fact that Aunty Wynn and I would acquire this bottle of liquid from a local veterinarian—a man who, I imagined, treated Uncle Cliff's horse, visited on the region's dairy cows and local dogs and cats, even that goat atop its triangular house.

My mother's death had been reduced to the death of a family pet, livestock.

'Not all that long ago you could get a prescription,' Aunty Wynn said. 'Now, unfortunately, only vets have access.'

'How do we know how much we need?' I asked.

I'd already made it clear that I would be there when we collected the drugs, and a horrifying new infographic had since appeared in my mind: NECESSARY DOSAGE: CAT, DOG, GOAT, COW, HORSE ... where did my mother slot in?

Aunty Wynn didn't exactly answer my question. 'Stephen's a very intelligent, reliable man, wouldn't you agree?' She looked to my mother for approval, as if they were discussing the quality of a pottle of tomatoes.

My mother attempted a thumbs up. '
And who's Stephen?' I said.

'The vet.'

Aunty Wynn had already given me this information, but I was confused and struggling to join the obvious dots. It wasn't a complicated plan. Aunty Wynn and I would be meeting the

vet on Monday morning, as my mother hadn't wanted the drugs in the house till she had told me her plan. The vet's name was Stephen, he owed Aunty Wynn some kind of a favour, and he was a very intelligent and reliable man. But how did they know what size dose my mother needed?

Now Aunty Wynn and my mother exchanged a knowing glance.

'What?' I asked.

'What?' Aunty Wynn replied. Then she heaved herself out of her La-Z-Boy and left the room.

I couldn't believe how casual—antagonistically casual!—they were both being. What didn't occur to me then was that they had had weeks, maybe months, to come to terms with this plan, and now they were on the final leg of the relay. I couldn't look at it the same way because I was still floundering around on the starting blocks.

'What was that look about?' I asked my mother. I sounded like the whiny kid left jumping in piggy-in-the-middle.

My mother smiled strangely, almost greedily. There was something they didn't want to share with me—an old nugget of gossip, something said in confidence. Maybe I didn't need to know, maybe it had nothing to do with the facts of my mother's death, but I felt left out all the same.

'Here.' Having returned, Aunty Wynn handed me the slim book from my mother's bedside table. 'This will give you some facts.'

The book looked like some self-published New Age atrocity. The cover image was a wild seascape with heavy clouds that had been fractured by godlike rays of a setting sun, which had then been confused by a multitude of purple tints and five different fonts. A large 'Restricted' sticker, like the kind you might find on an X-rated DVD, was affixed to the bottom right corner.

'You want me to read this?' I said. 'Are you kidding?'

I turned the book over in my hands. It looked as if it had been designed using the kind of paint and photo programme that comes free with PCs.

'The Nembutal chapter,' Aunty Wynn said.

'Mum?' I asked.

She returned a slow, loose nod.

We were talking about my mother's life, yet this was some serious DIY situation my mother and Aunty Wynn had going on. I thumbed through the handbook, my chest increasingly tight, as Aunty Wynn changed the topic of conversation to the new chlorination system at the pool where she swam, and, appearing equally relaxed, my mother let her hands hang limply over the end of her armrests.

I would have to get reading—how else could I be prepared for all the ways this thing could go wrong?

The Sunday Before

1

It was only just after seven o'clock but Aunty Wynn and Uncle Cliff were already awake and sitting silently at the kitchen table. They were each nursing a mug of milky tea and a slice of no-brand brown toast—Marmite for Uncle Cliff, marmalade for Aunty Wynn. The electric heater was cranked up to maximum and making loud gurgling noises.

'Good morning,' Aunty Wynn said. She was in unnervingly good spirits.

Out the kitchen window, in the dim morning light, I could just make out the girl from the day before back up on the trampoline. As she was jumping she was holding herself rigid like a statue, her arms at her sides, her long stringy hair gently whipping around her face like tendrils on a departing jellyfish. It didn't look fun—it looked like punishment. The radio was turned to a talk show: jittery voices still discussing the David Bain compensation claim.

'How did you sleep?' Aunty Wynn asked.

'I slept okay,' I said, though I hadn't. For an instant I'd heard my mother's warmth and gravel in Aunty Wynn's question—it made me drop my guard.

'And look at your socks,' Aunty Wynn said.

The socks had cats on them. They were a gift from Aunty Wynn herself a couple of Christmases earlier. I was also wearing the T-shirt, cardigan and jeans from the day before, which I

had slept in—badly. Actually I couldn't be sure I'd slept at all. I'd been having a tense, repetitive dream about the goat we had extracted on Saturday afternoon, but in my dream the goat was swinging from its collar, the tree its gallows. Then I'd realised I wasn't dreaming, that I was lying awake and *thinking* about that goat—its dirty undulating rump, its bleats increasing, waning, increasing, over and over.

Aunty Wynn's eyes were stuck on my feet. 'That's wonderful,' she said. Then she sighed, heavy with nostalgia, as if my sweaty cat socks were something precious.

I stepped up to the kitchen counter where the toaster was waiting, a bag of bread open beside it. I'd half expected Aunty Wynn to go off without me and meet Stephen the vet for the drug exchange a day early. A small part of me was disappointed she hadn't, and acknowledging this made me feel sheepish.

Before switching off the light the previous night, I'd found out how much Nembutal my mother would need to kill herself. It was all there in Aunty Wynn's suicide handbook. There were two options—one sterile, one non-sterile. I was unsure what sterility had to do with it, but one of the liquids was clear and the other was green. I'd written down all the numbers too. I was thinking about all of this while I leaned against the kitchen counter and listened to the toaster timer whirr.

So why did my aunty and uncle look like nothing new was going on, like it was an ordinary Sunday morning? Uncle Cliff reading some horse-themed newsletter, mousing at his toast, his tea now drained? Aunty Wynn making a list on a lilac-coloured notepad, her cup of tea firmly gripped in her free hand, her plate only crumbs? When was the last time I'd sat with my mother in our kitchen, bent over our toast and tea just like this? It had been nice. I hadn't realised how nice.

'When are we meeting your vet pal again?' I asked. I wanted a reaction, to stir up the calm, I guess.

It worked. Uncle Cliff flinched but didn't look up from his newsletter. Aunty Wynn peered at me, her eyes small with unease. She didn't want to discuss that subject while she was drinking her morning tea, penning her morning list.

'Tomorrow,' she said, brusquely. 'The crack of dawn.'

My toast popped. 'Good,' I said, digging my butter knife deep into the Marmite jar until it hit the bottom with an audible *thack*.

I felt like I'd achieved a fresh upper hand. It was a puerile and selfish way to get the day moving, but it invigorated me all the same.

Uncle Cliff turned the page of his newsletter. Aunty Wynn swigged deeply from her mug. And the girl on the trampoline was still bouncing in her unsettling corpse-like trance, while the man on the radio made a redundant stand for Bain's guilt. He's the only one who could've done it, he said, the only one who could've handled that rifle. But he also sounded empathetic, his tone suggesting that he might have done the same, he might have killed them all, too, if he had been in those shoes.

I took my toast and tea to my mother's room and sat cross-legged on the end of her bed, just as I'd done on weekend mornings when I was a child and our house was as cold as this house. The electric heater in my mother's room had just been switched on and was gurgling like the one in the kitchen. My mother was awake, propped up, with a brown and yellow scarf tied around her head. The curtains were drawn wide. Though the window was heavy with condensation and the sun was still coming up, the dolphin ornaments glittered obnoxiously.

'Aunty Wynn said she'll help you shower,' I said. 'When she's done with her tea.'

My mother nodded. I chewed on my toast, my cup of tea

nestled in the folds of my mother's duvet. Since re-entering my mother's room, my satisfaction of having ruffled Aunty Wynn had lost its sheen.

'What's that you're wearing?' I asked.

The headscarf was something new. There would be a story behind it, a reason for my mother to be wearing it. It made her look like a cancer patient. As expected, she had already prepared a response.

IT'S ART

'Art?' I said. I suddenly remembered I still hadn't sent her the photographs from the Mean Space exhibition. She'd known that would be the first thing that would pop into my head. And then there was Karl the gallery director, whom I'd barely considered since yesterday afternoon, but who now violently powered his way into my thoughts.

Karl, who had been offered a chance to prove his renewed commitment to his wife by submitting to a rigorous schedule of family time, curfews and sobering up, versus staying with me. In my more rational moments I'd not imagined a future for us beyond the gallery storage room, but when we were together I'd been able to trick myself into all of it: him leaving his wife, us getting married, me becoming a step-mother to his children, an apartment hung with really great paintings, a retired greyhound to keep us company the weeks we didn't have his kids. No matter how misguided that daydream was, the worst part was realising that at the end of it all I had nothing to leverage. No kids, no history, no security. All I had to offer was me, my unoriginal thesis, my lovely lean drumsticks.

It might not have been my mother's intent, but those two words— *it's art*—made me uneasy. Then I thought I knew where the scarf was from.

'Is that some of the silk I dyed in high school? With beetroot and onion skins?'

My mother gave me a perky thumbs up. Not to celebrate any

sentimentality, but because she trusted how bad the scarf made her look.

Though the scarf was silk, it was urine-yellow and potato-brown. It was my first and only attempt at natural dyeing, and no one had told me that beetroot dyed brown, not a lovely winey purple. My mother looked ill—even more ill than she was. She looked like she was ninety years old.

'It looks terrible,' I said.

She studied me then. A smile twitched at the corner of her mouth, and I felt both immensely content and immeasurably sad. Since she had started to lose her speech, there had been times that were so hard that I'd found myself, shamefully, feeling embarrassed—for her and myself. During those visits home, I'd avoided talking as much as possible, choosing instead to sulk around the house like I had as a teenager. But then more recently there were moments like this when, despite her not being able to talk, we could still take the piss out of each other like nothing had changed. We had loved each other this way for so long, the blanks, it turned out, could—when we both worked at it—be easily filled in.

Aunty Wynn started hollering from the kitchen. She was coming to help my mother with her shower, which was her way of telling me to finish up and get out of the road. I swept up the toast crumbs I'd dropped on the duvet and gathered my plate and cup. My mother had one more thing she wanted to show me, though—a note, mostly in bullet points.

TUESDAY
THE FINAL FROLIC
• FIND DAD'S LP PLAYER
• FLEETWOOD, TOM PETTY, LYNYRD SKYNYRD, JANIS, LINDA, BONNIE, STEVIE, UPBEAT JONI, SONG FROM BREAD AD, IRISH FOLK SONGS
 • FILL ROOM WITH FREESIAS

- CLEAR OUT DOLPHINS
- GNT TO GO

I examined the short list of final requests in silence.

'Joni Mitchell has an upbeat song?' I said finally.

I wasn't making a joke. I had no idea what she was talking about, and the Irish folk songs—that was something to do with Aunty Wynn, I thought bitterly. And did she expect me to find all of these on vinyl? I was the designated party planner for this morbid final frolic, and the promise of new failures loomed.

That high dry laugh of hers.

I couldn't even begin to fathom the very last request.

'Should I move the dolphins now?' I asked. It seemed like the easiest request to tick off the list, as well as the one I would get the most pleasure from.

My mother shook her head and gestured at the list, implying I should note it all down. As I started to type each bullet point into my phone, she looked over my shoulder at the ghastly ornaments. Her face was drawn into a frown—maybe she didn't want to see me copying down her final requests with so little effort? But even my typing was taking too long, so I stopped and photographed the list instead—I had to get out of there quickly and into the only bathroom before my mother had her shower.

No, I couldn't reconcile that list of requests with my mother being alive, the two of us together in that room. It was as if I were already organising her funeral, as if Tuesday had come and gone and I'd missed it all. And my guts, and then my bowels, were suddenly trembling with a brand new violence.

She could walk, very slowly and with wobbles, with the support of her four-wheeled walker. I watched from outside Bethany's old bedroom, where I'd spent the night—accompanied by

the boxes full of my mother's possessions—as Aunty Wynn followed her, both hands extended and hovering near the small of my mother's back. They were heading to the bathroom, which I'd exited only a few minutes before.

I should have felt a surge of good feeling towards Aunty Wynn then. She was in nurse mode, but there was tenderness in the way she shuffled behind my mother, as if she were a young mother shuffling behind an unsteady toddler. While I am grateful now, at the time I could only think about how frail my mother looked, no longer the tall, broad-shouldered, boisterous woman I'd always known. And I felt jealous. Because that should have been me following her, taking care of her, being her number one. She had never wanted it, though, had never wanted me to move from Auckland and my study and my work and the gallery to take care of her in our Wellington home. She had flat-out refused. She had been aggressive about it: 'I can't deal with the thought of you having to see all of the bad and disgusting bits. You're still my child.'

So here we were. I sniffed deeply. The embarrassments of my own body were leaking into the hallway, though neither my mother nor Aunty Wynn would say anything. Maybe it was because my mother and I had not lived with boys for any consistent amount of time, but lighthearted jokes about bodily functions had never been a regular feature in our home.

My confident, brazen mother, always ready to laugh: the look on her face when she accidentally let one rip! Her legs would comically buckle inwards at the knees, her cheeks would flush pink, and she would put her hand to her mouth, very Victorian, and say, 'Oops,' followed by, 'Excuse me,' after which she would leave the room.

At the pool I'd gotten a taste of the joy that boys get out of our human grossness, which was why I wondered whether spending so long in an oestrogen-only zone was the reason my mother could not have imagined—compared with her sister,

the nurse, whose job it was to know—her daughter having to witness things so personal and disgusting up close.

Though I had. Once.

It was about six months earlier. My mother's speech had been getting increasingly muddy, though she could still eat and move about on her own. I'd returned home for a few nights. We were watching one of our favourite disaster movies, *The Day After Tomorrow*, and we'd got to the part where the kids barricade themselves against the pack of wolves. We'd seen the movie many times, but I was quietly, nervously wringing my hands, while my mother growled at the TV, 'They should get out of there. The wolves, the wolves!' Then she went quiet. Her eyes bugged out, and she looked away from the TV and instead began staring at her lap, at the folds of her large woollen sweater, and at her tights, a jazzy pair with bright geometric prints.

I was still unaware anything was wrong when she finally spoke. Without looking at me she said, flatly, 'Can you please give me a minute?'

'What?' I said, not really listening.

She picked up the remote, paused the movie. 'Erin, just leave the room.' She sounded flustered, angry.

By the time I reached my bedroom I'd figured out what was going on. I felt hot with shame. I started to weep a little—like a child who had been scolded. I tried to pull myself together, but I remained standing just inside my bedroom doorway. I held my breath while I tried to make out where my mother was: now in the bathroom, now in her bedroom, now back in the living room, now in the laundry. I was trying to figure out when I should return to the living room and...do what?

We did meet back in the living room. And even though the couch was missing one of its seat cushions, and my mother was wearing a different pair of jazzy tights and a fresh grey sweatshirt, we both acted like nothing had happened.

Eventually, during another visit home, she and I had the

conversation about what she would do when she could no longer take care of herself, which was when she had put her foot down about my role. She would pay for an in-home nurse, first to come and help, and then to stay with her full-time, and that was what had happened, and eventually I made some peace with it. But then, months later, seemingly out of the blue, she informed me that she would be moving out of our home and back to the house where she had grown up so Aunty Wynn could take care of her instead. When she explained this plan, I assumed she was joking. I offered a hearty laugh and said, 'Nice one, Mum. What a nightmare.'

She looked at me calmly, without smiling. She explained it mostly in terms of finances—she had eaten through most of her savings paying for her increasingly demanding in-home care—but she also made an offhand comment about wanting to return home. 'Like a salmon,' she said. 'Minus the spawning.' She had never before mentioned wanting to go back to the Moore family house, which led me to believe it was just about the money. I made sure she knew that I didn't care about the money, in case that was a contributing factor, and I told her many times that she should stay, that she should be in her home, that I would move to help and be there with her. It didn't make any difference. Or I didn't fight hard enough.

Standing in the Moore family house now and watching Aunty Wynn do her thing, I felt newly guilty about the whole situation. We were nearing the end and I realised that all this time I could have been doing this—I could have been the one taking care of her. My mother and I could have reached this point together. I should have put *my* foot down. I should have taken over, stepped up. I would have figured it out, wouldn't I?

I wish I'd been tougher. More generous, less frightened. I wish I'd been a different person. Not my mother's daughter, I guess.

Now as I listened to the sound of my mother's leopard-print

slippers and Aunty Wynn's Ugg boots shuffling in unison along the wooden floorboards, accompanied by the squeak-squeak of the four rubber wheels of my mother's walker, I thought: That is the exact sound of creeping death. I tried to breathe deeply but could only manage a shallow suck of air.

My mother went into the bathroom. Then, as if she had once again read my thoughts, Aunty Wynn threw me a pained look of sympathy, and I averted my eyes.

On the wall beside me, above another shelf of uncracked Reader's Digest books—mystery novels, many mint-condition Asian and Asian-fusion cookbooks, one title on Nordic cuisine, a large volume called *Adventures in Microwave Cooking*—was a row of black-and-white family photos. I'd noticed them in passing the day before. Now I lingered. For the most part I wasn't familiar with the people pictured, though I guessed they were my grandfather and grandmother when they were young, and their parents who had lived in this house before them. Yet one photo caught my eye. It was of my mother and Aunty Wynn as teenagers.

'Hey, Mum,' I said.

But Aunty Wynn had already closed the bathroom door behind them.

In the photo they were standing on a beach wearing matching togs with lightning bolts across their chests, and striped life-saving beanies tied in neat cotton bows under their chins. I'd forgotten they had both been surf-lifesavers as well as swimmers. They looked as if they had just emerged from the sea—they were dripping wet, their faces bright. Aunty Wynn's arm was wrapped around my mother's shoulders. They were both grinning. No, beaming.

I could hear them laughing on the other side of the bathroom door: Aunty Wynn with that boom of a laugh, my mother with her charred shriek. It made me wonder whether the real reason

my mother had wanted to come back was simply because she missed her sister.

Growing up in Wellington, I'd never much swum in the sea. It was too cold for the public to bother much, either, so surf-lifesavers weren't in high demand. I felt certain I would have followed the family tradition if my mother had never left this place, if I'd been born up here where it was warmer. I took a small comfort in the fact that that wasn't the case. In my opinion, the only natural response to sea swimming is a paralysed dread of whatever else might be swimming in there too. But the two Moore sisters—tall and svelte with shoulders you could really hang a coat off—standing side by side in that photo, they looked entirely fearless.

2

'I saw the oven bags,' I said.

I was counting out the $1 and 50c coins I needed for the swimming pool entry fee when I decided to say it. Aunty Wynn overtook me, flashing her annual pass to the lifeguard. For a moment it looked as though she was going to walk away from me to avoid responding to what I'd said. But she didn't. She waited for me on the other side of the turnstile.

'What's that you say?' she asked innocently.

I inhaled deeply. The smell of chlorine was crushing, but I liked it, an old friend. 'I saw the oven bags in Bethany's cupboard.'

'Oh really?'

When Aunty Wynn had mentioned she would be going to the pool after lunch, and would I like to come, I'd answered so quickly and with my mouth so full of Marmite and cheese sandwich that she hadn't understood, so I'd repeated myself: 'Yes, please.' Whatever bad feelings I'd been stewing on that morning were instantly overridden by my need for a swim. I was grateful for the offer. So grateful that, while Aunty Wynn had assisted my mother with her own lunch, I'd felt inspired to tick off the first item on my mother's wish list: my grandfather's record player.

Not surprisingly, it turned out to be no more. At least, it wasn't in the garage or the cupboard in Bethany's old bedroom—the only places it could be, according to Aunty Wynn. However, I had found something in Bethany's cupboard: a collection of Glad oven bags, the large kind in which you might roast a big chook or a turkey. They had strips of elastic and tape circling

their openings. There were three in total, in varying stages of elastic and tape construction, and they had been stashed with a coil of plastic tubing. They had not been accidentally put there from the kitchen. I knew what they were because the night before I'd ended up reading a lot of the suicide handbook Aunty Wynn had given me. Including the chapter on hypoxic death.

In the women's changing room I placed the ancient Pak'nSave bag, bursting with my swimming gear, undies and borrowed towel, on the wooden bench. Aunty Wynn unzipped her large purple gym bag and pretended to rummage around inside it—using her hands to dig haphazardly as if tossing one of her iceberg lettuce salads. She was trying to figure out what she wanted to say about my discovery.

I had my togs on under my clothes so I stripped off my cardigan, T-shirt, shoes and socks, and undid the top button of my jeans. I felt tense, and the feeling was made worse by the stench of chlorine, which since my competitive swimming days had been both welcoming and anxiety-provoking. I'd spent the whole car ride to the pool psyching myself up to say something about the oven bags.

When I'd realised what they were, I'd had to sit on Bethany's old bed to catch my breath. I was having difficulty catching it again now. The image of a scarecrow, its head made out of a plastic bag, kept appearing in my mind. The plastic bag had muddy-coloured eyes and red lips drawn on, and my disgusting silk scarf wrapped around its temple—a crude and terrified rendition of my mother. Crucified.

Now that we were on the edge of discussing the bags, I felt no relief. I slouched on the seat and leaned against the wall. The dark- blue painted cinder blocks were cold and damp.

'I get the feeling,' I said, not looking at Aunty Wynn as I spoke, 'that you left them for me to find. On purpose.'

She was suddenly standing beside me wearing nothing

but her chicken-coloured tracksuit jacket, which only just, but thankfully, covered her pubic area. I was stunned by her nakedness, the surprising shape of her pale muscular thighs. I narrowed my gaze at the three shower nooks across the room—there was a spray of hair climbing up the wall of the middle one, and an ombré of green and black mould on the bottom of each plastic curtain—while out the corner of my eye, I tried not to watch as she bent over and put one foot and now the other through the leg holes of her turquoise togs, letting out a sharp sucking noise and now a groan, and wriggled her way in. She started to unzip her tracksuit jacket, but stopped. Her glasses had misted up with condensation and she probably couldn't see more than a foot in front of her.

'It's true,' she said, her tone restrained, even coy, and made stranger by her temporary blindness. 'The Moore women are craftier than we look.'

I took that to mean she *had* stashed the oven bags where I would find them. But why? It was horrifying to have to picture my mother dying with a plastic bag over her head. And a bag for roasting poultry! Because of the presence of plastic tubing, I gathered that my mother had considered using helium—a method rated highly on the suicide handbook's peacefulness scale. It didn't matter. I could only think of all the episodes of *SVU* I'd watched—the ones where a young woman fights for her life as a semi-opaque plastic shopping bag is forced down against her nose and mouth, her expression wild with terror. Had my mother imagined this too?

On the other hand, what I had just *known* the day before, when I could not argue with my mother about her choice to leave, when I was reluctant but ready to accept her decision, could now be firmly proved: she wasn't kidding around with this. If she had truly considered this option then she *had* thought it through; she *was* serious.

'Initially, I put the oven bags back in the kitchen drawer,' Aunty Wynn said, her lenses still clouded. 'They were perfectly fine, still useable.'

'Then you thought you'd move them to Bethany's cupboard?' I asked.

'The thought of cooking with them made me feel funny,' she said. 'But I couldn't bring myself to throw them out. The waste.' She shook her head. She was unconvinced by her own lie.

It didn't matter that this was no longer what my mother was planning. I'd become freshly overwhelmed by the picture of her dying this way. 'I don't want to think about Mum with one of those bags on her head,' I said.

'Get away from that wall,' Aunty Wynn said. She wagged her hand, indicating that I shouldn't be leaning back against the cold cinderblocks.

I did what she said. I put my elbows on my knees and stared at the floor. Aunty Wynn sat down on the bench beside me and took up the same position. She sat so that our shoulders were touching. It was intimate, only the two of us in that chlorine-soaked room. Usually that would have mortified me, sitting side by side with Aunty Wynn like that, as if we were alone at a confessional, but for a moment I forgot everything that maddened me about her, and I enjoyed our closeness. I felt like I could tell her things. What did I want to tell her?

'I know what you're saying.' She spoke first. 'She couldn't do it anyway. Couldn't thread the elastic herself.'

She sounded not only resigned, but also relieved to the point of exhaustion. And for the first time, it occurred to me that everything I was struggling with—the paralysing images of my mother dead or dying, and the logistics of the solution she had settled on, where she would be more or less tranquilised like a farm animal—Aunty Wynn might be struggling with too.

'I couldn't picture her having the strength,' I said, 'to keep the

bag from violently suffocating her while the helium leaked in.'

Aunty Wynn turned to face me. Her glasses had de-fogged. Her eyes flickered with intelligence, that Moore-woman craftiness.

'So you read the book?'

There it was—her reason for stashing the oven bags where I could find them. It had been a test. To see how committed I was. To find out how far in I was willing to wade.

'I did,' I said.

What came next shouldn't have surprised me. I'd vaguely wondered how Aunty Wynn had managed to convince such an apparently honourable man as Stephen the vet to supply the drugs for my mother, but I'd not thought about specifics. That was more than I could get my head around. I'd also assumed my mother knew, whatever the story was, and that if she was okay with it, then I would have to be okay with it. It turned out my mother didn't know. And now Aunty Wynn was desperate to share.

'Your mum knows Stephen and I used to be involved,' she said. She lingered weirdly on the middle of involved—in*vol*ved—as if she were still figuring out the meaning of the word. 'A long time ago, when we were just kids really. What she doesn't know is that we were still in*vol*ved'—she did it again—'up until all of this happened.'

I took 'all of this' to mean my mother's illness, her impending exit.

'Even after he got married,' Aunty Wynn said, her words increasingly tinged with sadness. 'Though we stopped seeing each other when his three kiddies first came along, and while Bethany's father was in the picture, but then. We shouldn't have.' She was shaking her head, though half-heartedly. 'But we

did.' Now she began to whisper, though no one else had entered the changing room. 'That's how we're getting the Nembutal.'

I didn't fully understand. 'Isn't that what we talked about last night?'

'Your mum thinks he's just doing me a favour. She believes he's a *jolly* nice man doing a *jolly* nice thing for an old friend.'

Aunty Wynn stressed the hell out of those *jolly*s—her bitterness was plain. She turned and looked at me, and I was surprised to see there were tears in her eyes. She sniffed, dug into her tracksuit pocket and pulled out a clean cotton hankie, neatly pressed. She unfolded it, wiped it delicately across the tip of her nose.

'I was happy for her to believe that. She's been through so much already.' She took a moment to refold her hankie and stuff it back in her pocket. 'I said to Stephen that I would have to tell his wife about us if he didn't help. Because'—she sniffed lightly, put her hand to her pocket as if to retrieve the hankie again, but didn't—'otherwise he wasn't going to help.'

Her eyes were wide with disbelief. It wasn't disbelief that some guy wasn't willing to break the law, but disbelief that Stephen the vet, whom she had been secretly seeing for however many decades, whom she had obviously been in love with, wasn't willing to break the law for her. Stephen the vet had broken her heart.

'I guess that makes me a blackmailer,' she said.

'Yes,' I said stupidly. The wind had been knocked out of me.

Though I was a little impressed—I'd never imagined Aunty Wynn capable of conducting a long-term illicit affair—there was now another level of criminality to what we were doing. Not only were we helping my mother kill herself, using drugs that weren't meant for human use, we were also acquiring the drugs through blackmail. The whole thing was looking more and more like the plot of a French farce, except it wasn't funny.

And I knew for certain then that there was no way this could come off without a hitch. One of us, if not all of us, would be going to prison.

'Mum doesn't know any of this?' I asked.

Aunty Wynn shook her head.

'Only you, me, and this Stephen?'

She nodded.

'Anyone else?' I asked.

She shook her head.

'I'm not sure you needed to rope me in.' As soon as I said this, I wished I hadn't.

Aunty Wynn's round face flushed. It was guilt, yes, but also hurt. She had hoped I would understand.

I didn't completely then, but I do now.

My mother had been through a lot, but this kind of drama—the illicit affair, the betrayals, the blackmail!—wouldn't she have loved to know? Yes, and that was why Aunty Wynn hadn't told her the truth. She didn't want to risk my mother making fun of her—she wasn't ready to laugh about it. Why did she trust me, then? A day earlier, there was nothing I would have enjoyed more than to run to my mother with this story. The mileage we would have gotten out of this affair! But a lot had changed since Saturday, even in the time since I'd entered the swimming pool changing room. I couldn't make fun of Aunty Wynn's failure when it was framed by a readiness to sacrifice her relationship with this man for my mother. And this, I think, was why she let me in on the details. To prove to me how much she loved her sister, with the hope that I might eventually let her in too.

I also think she needed someone to bear witness. She was tired of going it alone.

▲

I was eighteen when I retired from competitive swimming. I stopped swimming completely—only visiting pools in my dreams, monotone anxiety dreams where shapes were flattened out like a Suprematist experiment, and the water was too thin so my arms just spun, or I had no arms or legs and was merely a large uncoordinated shard of my former athletic self. It was immediately after I returned from Wellington, the visit where I'd learned about my mother's diagnosis, that I bought a membership to one of Auckland's inner-city pools. I'd swum there six mornings a week, every week since. It was the only thing in the last year and a bit that had given me any real comfort.

And that was why, despite everything that had passed between us in the quiet damp of the women's changing room, Aunty Wynn and I could find the energy to get into the pool.

At the end of each lane were plastic signs announcing the following: water-walking, slow, medium, fast. I stood on the pool deck beside the starting block of the fast centre lane, and stuffed stray wisps of my grapefruit-coloured hair into my swim cap. Though the pool was indoor, heated, and a full twenty-five metres, the tiles beneath my feet were slick with scum, the lane-ropes were noticeably faded and gap-toothed, and there was definitely bird shit on the lane three starting block. Still, I'd swum in worse. There were a few others swimming, including two women in the water-walking lane, whom Aunty Wynn drew into a circle around her as soon as she entered the water. My lane was thankfully empty.

Now Aunty Wynn looked up from her trio of cycling and yakking women and flapped her large pale arm at me. Of the two women with her, a Pacific Island woman who was much younger than Aunty Wynn, and who I assumed was Aunty Wynn's nurse pal, gave me a cheerful wave, as if we were already old friends. Aunty Wynn was grinning proudly. Nothing from

the changing room registered on her face. She had spent her whole life concealing her feelings—she was a pro at it.

I waved to the group as coolly as possible. I already had my goggles on, and had been bracing myself to dive in, but now I needed to reposition my goggles—a nervous habit, made worse by knowing that Aunty Wynn and her mates were watching me. I took a moment to run my fingers around the inside of the hard plastic to defog them once more, then repositioned them over my eyes with the right sucking sound. Without looking at my audience, I breathed in sharply and dived into the pool with a casual loping arch.

Immediately my goggles flooded with water.

I didn't surface to adjust them—I couldn't concede the failure. Before our conversation in the changing room, it would have been enough to say that I didn't want Aunty Wynn to have the upper hand of witnessing such a shoddy dive. Since her confession, I felt something different—that I needed to prove myself to her. My opinion of her had changed, and now I felt some pride in the fact that she trusted me, that I was the one she had let in on her secret. It made me feel important, wanted. And that was enough to keep me swimming.

Swimming with goggles full of water is much worse than swimming with no goggles. It was impossible to see even when turning my head to breathe. The pale blue tiles in the pool, the dirty cream-coloured tiles around the pool, the flesh-coloured walls, and the high windows shot with that cold, deep blue June sky all swirled into a disorienting tie-dyed vision. At the end of my first length I tumble-turned so close to the wall that my ankles hit the outside ledge of the pool. But I didn't stop—I pushed off as best as I could, hoping Aunty Wynn hadn't seen.

When I was in competitive training, I would often imagine spectators watching me from the stands. Not crowds of people, but a select one or two—people I wanted to impress. It made me swim faster. Before his wife found out about us, I'd

imagined Karl observing me from the faded plastic seats on the side of the pool— sitting with his legs crossed in expensive wool pants, his balding spot shining in the humid pool light, and with every one of my strokes becoming more and more blown away by my strength, agility and sexiness.

When I was a teenager it was my mother up there in the stands. For real. Every day she watched the first half of my morning training, and the second half of my evening sessions. Even though she had been a swimmer too, it was boring viewing so she knitted while she watched: colourful slippers that I still wear, and big ugly scarves of coarse lambswool that I could never wear because they made my face and neck itch.

I pulled up at the opposite end of the pool from where Aunty Wynn and her friends were slowly turning over. I was struggling to catch my breath. It wasn't the swimming—I'd only swum three lengths. It wasn't even because I was being blinded by chlorinated water. Thinking about my mother in that way—watching me from above!—it was too much. I removed my goggles. What did I need to do now? I needed to complete everything on my mother's list and not be flippant about her last wishes—if she wanted upbeat Joni Mitchell and freesias, then that was what she would get. I needed to find out exactly what the vial of Nembutal should look like, because there was no way we could trust Stephen the vet. I also needed to find a way to be kinder to Aunty Wynn.

Goggles back on, I pushed off the wall. My head down, my arms locked, my eyes trained on those rows and rows of pale blue tiles, I exhaled out my nose. Though when I broke the surface of the water I didn't immediately turn for air.

3

While I was swimming, Karl left me a voicemail message.

'It's me,' he said. 'I wanted to call and check in. Friday wasn't the best, eh?' He sighed deeply, but there was a pleasurable element to it, as if he were enjoying himself. 'Give me a call when you get this.' Before he hung up, he stayed on the line for a few noiseless seconds.

At another time I would have been stoked to receive such a message. I would have interpreted it to mean there were Erin and Karl instalments to come. I would have played the message multiple times, examined every angle. I would have stared at Karl's number and not dialled. I would have drunk a bottle of wine, a third of another, and then dialled. Anything might have happened after that. Though now, as I listened to the message again, while I hung my togs and towel and Aunty Wynn's togs and towel on the washing line to dry, I felt like a creep. I hadn't forgotten how pathetic I'd felt when I'd realised I had nothing to leverage, nothing substantial to offer Karl for him to choose me. But I was also experiencing a period of clarity. A married father? Erin, really?

Riding high on my new clear-headedness, I slid my phone back in my jeans pocket and surveyed the backyard.

On one side, the yard had a chest-high wooden fence that butted against the property with the trampoline and small children. The back fence, its perpendicular counterpart, was only waist-high—five wide- set wires. On the other side of that fence was what remained of the Moore family farm: empty, scrubby paddocks. In the distance, at the edge of a ridge, was the spare, windswept outline of a grove of mānuka trees. Beyond that: denser native bush, the Kaipara harbour.

68

Back inside the yard was the original garage, which had been converted into a self-contained sleep-out. That was where Uncle Cliff lived, though I'd never been inside. Next to the sleep-out were his vegetable gardens. Uncle Cliff was there, too, poking around. He had constructed the gardens out of old tractor tyres—there were half a dozen of them organised in a semicircle. I remembered from my last visit, back when I was a kid, something about the thick rubber of the tyres helping to keep the soil warm. Despite being this far north, the temperatures could drop impressively in winter. That afternoon, although it was only early June, and the sun was out, the sky an electric blue, there was a sharp chill to the air. I doubted the togs and towels would get close to dry.

Uncle Cliff was bent over a cluster of cabbages. He took out a short, sharp knife and cut one off at the root. It was a big purple and green beauty. He lovingly turned it around in his hands, a smile twitching on his usually composed face.

'What're you growing?' I asked. I could clearly see they were cabbages, but I was itching to listen to Karl's message again and I needed a distraction.

'This one's called a January King,' Uncle Cliff said. He was wearing a pair of navy overalls zipped all the way up, and a green and white trucker hat. His half-moon glasses hung, as always, on their fluorescent-yellow cord. He lobbed the cabbage to me like a rugby ball.

I caught it in an uncoordinated hug. 'Cool,' I said, tentatively turning it around, doing my best to admire it as he had. I hated to think what Aunty Wynn might have planned for it.

'I'm going to give most of these to a mate,' Uncle Cliff said. 'She makes a bloody good kimchi. Even with this variety.' He looked incredulous, as if the idea of kimchi made from this kind of cabbage was madness.

He took the cabbage back, smiling broadly.

'So you guys eat the rest of these veges?' I asked, gesturing

across the six tractor-tyre gardens. I was thinking about what we'd eaten for dinner the previous night: mashed potatoes, peas, none of it homegrown.

'Most of it I sell at the local market,' he said, walking towards the fence at the back of the yard and resting an elbow on one of the sturdier wooden posts. I followed him. 'It's nothing special, no fancy greenhouse,' he said, and nodded behind the sleep-out. 'But you'd be surprised what I can grow.'

On the other side of the fence were maybe two dozen more tractor-tyre gardens I hadn't noticed earlier. The scene looked like a site-specific art installation. Some of the gardens didn't look any different from the six inside the yard, but many more were covered in short plastic teepees of varying colours—to protect the produce from the wind and birds, I guessed.

Uncle Cliff had plenty to say about his vegetable gardens and the local market. He explained how his friend sold the kimchi for fifteen dollars a jar to the Aucklanders passing through the market on their weekend drives. He became extremely animated at the mention of swindling all those city folks. 'Fifteen bucks!' he said. 'Can you believe it?'

Initially I'd wondered what Uncle Cliff knew of Aunty Wynn's affair, or of tomorrow's meeting with Stephen the vet, but the more we talked, the more certain I felt that there was very little he didn't know. He had always seemed so quiet and uninteresting, even dopey, during our annual family lunches. I recalled his spaced-out staring at the kitchen table the night before. But, though I couldn't figure out whether it was a wilful act or a defence mechanism, underneath that quietness he was a lot more like my mother and Aunty Wynn than I'd realised.

I enjoyed talking to him. In some ways, I felt like we were properly meeting for the first time, and the more we talked, the more I felt like a person who belonged in that yard. Though I also had an ulterior motive: once I'd learned of his local market

connections, I'd hoped he would be able to help me with something on my mother's wish list.

'Do you know where I could get freesias this time of year?' I asked.

He waved his hand, implying it was no problem. 'Yeah, yeah. They're not perfect in June, but we can do that. We can do that. I know a guy.'

I know a guy. That's what he said.

And so it was done. Uncle Cliff would make some calls and arrange to collect the freesias Monday afternoon. It was almost as if he had already fixed it, well in advance of our conversation.

Ticking off one of my mother's requests was a small win. I immediately destroyed that good feeling with another listen of Karl's message. With each play, I inserted more empathy and longing into his voice. After I'd endured another run of those final few seconds of silence before he hung up—what was he thinking about, had he meant to say something else, what?—I lingered over the call button.

I was making my way down the front drive. Aunty Wynn's internet connection was weak and patchy—reliable enough for my mother to send me emails, but not to download the music she had requested— so I was heading to Bethany's. Apparently her connection was better. Aunty Wynn had given me a key to the house and a sheet of her lilac-coloured notepaper on which she'd written directions for navigating the subdivision. She had explained the route in overly detailed steps. *Walk carefully along the grassy verge. Watch out for cars and trucks!* and *Take a hard right into Buttercup Green. Stay on the right side of the path as Joel Henry's bull terrier (house #5) might be off his leash.* The reverse side contained a map, including a square for each house I would pass on my route. Despite its proximity

to the subdivision, the Moore family house still had its original driveway and street address, so to get to Bethany's I would have to make an elongated U shape. First I would have to walk down the long gravel driveway then along the main road, before heading back up Buttercup Green, which I could see clearly from where I was currently standing on the driveway, before veering off into Freshfields Meadow. All the roads in the subdivision had similar new-nostalgia names.

Clutching a thin hope that Karl still wanted me, I was a worry of distraction walking down that driveway. I also feared returning his call—concerned that I might suddenly turn desperate and say something needy that I couldn't take back and that I didn't necessarily even mean. I didn't trust myself to come out on top. And that's what I was afraid of most: losing more than I already had. So when, for no reason that I can remember, I lifted the notepaper containing Aunty Wynn's directions to my nose and sniffed, I guess I was expecting it to smell sweet, maybe comforting, like the tiny purple and green lilacs in each corner of the sheet. Instead, it smelled of mothballs and something sharp. That woke me up—the surprise of how much it smelled like aged cheddar. It was like inhaling toxic smelling salts. It made me remember what was actually important: music for my mother, more information about the drugs, and helping to keep this rickety, poorly manned boat on an even keel. With these things at the front of my mind again, I could let Karl slide to the back.

I walked quickly and with purpose along the main road, being careful, as per Aunty Wynn's directions, to stay on the uneven grassy verge and out of the way of oncoming traffic: a total of one hatchback and two utes. Inside the subdivision, Buttercup Green and Freshfields Meadow were tightly sealed, with rolling

sidewalks and too many streetlamps all cast in a ridiculous dark green old-timey style.

Those neat wavy roads and too-similar houses had been plonked down, with little consideration, right there in the middle of the countryside, off an unsealed main road, kilometres from anything, patchy mānuka trees and ugly paddocks on the periphery. Who would want to live here? Also, where was everyone? It was a Sunday afternoon in the middle of a holiday weekend, and the subdivision was deserted. Many of the houses—some with curtains, some without—appeared dark inside. Every yard had been planted out impressively, but most of the trees and shrubs were small and bare. Maybe it was the greyness of the day, but the place didn't feel fresh and new and *growing in*. It felt completely devoid of life.

I picked up my speed.

'Hello? Erin?'

Across the road, two doors down from where Aunty Wynn's map told me Bethany's house was, a woman was standing in her front yard between two waist-high shrubs. She was waving at me like we were old mates.

Though I couldn't immediately pinpoint why, the sight of her exasperated me. I slowed a little, but didn't stop. In the Wellington neighbourhood where I grew up, I couldn't recall a single time a neighbour had called my name and waved at me from their front yard. Was that why people moved to these places, for some kind of nosey community feel? Out there, in the middle of nowhere, it seemed like a huge, idiotic gamble.

'I'm Cecilia,' she called. 'Your aunty's friend, from the pool.' She pointed at herself with her thumb, something a primary school teacher would do. 'Most people call me Lia.'

Despite the temperature out, she was wearing a T-shirt and tiny cotton shorts—hot pink with a frayed white cord, her hair tied up in a high shiny bun. Now that she was outside of the

swimming pool, I could see how young she was—my age or thereabouts.

I smiled and waved awkwardly. Did she expect me to cross the road?

'I saw you this morning,' she said. 'You're a proper swimmer. Like your aunty, yes? Not like me!' She did a few example strokes that were more like a windmill action than freestyle. She laughed loudly and sincerely. She was a ball of big, positive gestures.

I stepped into the road, but continued my beeline for Bethany's front door.

'Your aunty said I should keep an eye out for you.' She had her hands on her hips now, the same way Aunty Wynn liked to stand when commanding the attention of a room. Except that in the case of Cecilia, or Lia, the gesture somehow made her appear welcoming.

'I'm heading to my cousin's to use her computer,' I said. 'The internet at the other house is too garbage.' I waved half-heartedly behind me. I had to raise my voice because of the distance I'd put between us.

'I know! I know!' Lia called. She had to lean all the way over her fence—a white-picket thing—so she could still see me. 'You like to come in for a cup of tea?'

At least, I think that's what she said. I'd already entered Bethany's front yard and was fumbling with the keys in the front door, doing my best not to listen, trying my hardest not to engage.

What was I afraid of?

Did I seem obviously afraid?

For the last year and a bit, I'd increasingly operated in select bubbles: a university bubble, a Mean Space bubble, a Mum-and-me bubble, and sometimes smaller bubbles for whomever I was sleeping with. I'd streamlined my social interactions to only the absolute necessities—whatever was needed to

complete the task at hand. Because of this, I'd fallen out of touch with friends. The thought of entering a strange woman's house for tea—I could already hear the uncomfortable chink of cup on saucer, see the embarrassment of biscuit crumbs spilled down the front of my cardigan—and the prospect that she might want to discuss something that wasn't directly related to how chapter three of my master's thesis was coming on, or whether I needed more screws to install those final paintings, was more than I could handle.

So I'd run away.

Now that I was standing on the other side of Bethany's front door, I felt both relieved and hot, as if I'd just returned from a run. As I caught my breath, I took in the room in front of me. On the wall opposite the front door was a giant poster of the Beatles—the zebra- crossing with the four of them striding in a line. The rest of the room—walls, carpet, couches, rug, curtains, light fixtures—were varying shades of unadorned cream and beige, like something out of a really depressing homewares catalogue.

I found the computer down the hall in Bethany's bedroom. It was sitting on what looked like an old kitchen table, surrounded by half a dozen vases crammed with dried flowers. She had more Beatles posters on the walls, a Jim Morrison banner, a lava lamp switched on, and a hat stand crammed with brightly patterned neck scarves. There was a birdcage, too, but I couldn't see a bird.

The personality of that bedroom was not how I remembered the Bethany of last year's Queen's Birthday lunch, who arrived at our Wellington home in a knee-length Megadeth T-shirt, her greasy bottle-black hair halfway down her back. I was vaguely curious about this new version of my cousin, but then I saw that the computer, when I woke it up, was locked, and that Aunty Wynn had failed, in all her organisational glory, to give me the password.

Bethany's bedroom had a strange smell—a confusing cross between weed and mouldy bread. While I waited for Aunty Wynn to return my call I headed to the kitchen and browsed the pantry. It was incredibly well stocked with canned foods, dry goods neatly labelled in uniform Tupperware containers, and packets of lunchbox snacks: chips, yoghurt-covered raisins, single-servings of crackers and cheese dip. It was a pantry fit for a bunker.

I had no doubt that Aunty Wynn did all of Bethany's shopping, so I helped myself to a family-sized bag of Twisties.

Through the French doors that led from the kitchen to the backyard I could see shrubs, still with their tags on, struggling against the far fence. There were a couple of lawn chairs, and an expensive-looking gas barbecue, though the focal point of that square of grass was a huge triangular frame made of two-by-four planks of wood. It was nearly as tall as the house. What was Bethany doing out there? Installing a giant version of Uncle Cliff's garden teepees? Making herself a hut? A jungle gym? A pagoda? Whatever it was, it didn't look professionally constructed, or stable.

Even after I'd spent long enough in the kitchen to demolish two thirds of the bag of chips, Aunty Wynn still hadn't called back. Throwing myself into those Twisties was the most freeing thing I'd done in a while, but I was starting to feel sick, and tired. I rolled up the rest of the bag and stashed it in my satchel. I didn't have time to waste, and yet here I was wasting it. I wasn't helping to steer this rickety boat. I was only a seasick crew member pulling haphazardly on some ropes—ropes that could have been connected to nothing. How would I have known?

When I walked back past Lia's house, she was nowhere to be seen.

4

I woke from my nap with my jaw clenched and my hands again balled into fists and crossed at my chest as if I was lying in a casket, minus any peacefulness. I looked at my phone—I'd only been out for twenty-five minutes, but I'd swiftly fallen into a shallow, worried sleep. I'd dreamed of Lia, of our awkward conversation, though I'd come off even worse in my dream—yelling at her 'Leave me alone!' and then running at full speed down the road, my arms flailing above my head like one of those inflatable noodle men outside car dealerships. The surge of real panic as I realised that was how I might have appeared to her, only marginally less strange, was what had woken me. That, and I could hear Aunty Wynn's voice booming down the hall.

'Remember how you collected all those knitting patterns?' she said, cheerful and mocking. 'And you couldn't even knit.'

She was in my mother's room. I pictured my mother on the other end of the exchange, silently laughing, her head thrown back against her pillow.

I poked my head around the doorway. My mother *was* silently laughing, her eyes shut, her head pitched back. While Aunty Wynn was joshing my mother—being a *hoot*—she was carefully loading her dolphin ornaments into a cardboard box lined with a hand towel. She was shifting the trinkets one at a time. Even the ones made of wood or rock, which were clearly not fragile and didn't need to be moved with two hands.

'I know this was your job, but I thought I'd help.' Aunty Wynn said this kindly, looking at me as she spoke. In her hands was

one of her least convincing specimens: a vague dolphin shape made from glued-together river stones, the glue very visible, and finished with plastic googly eyes. 'There's another box if you want to join in.' She nodded at the floor at the end of the bed. 'There's new shelves for them now. They'll have pride of place.'

What I wanted to say, or what the Erin of yesterday would have said, was, 'Why wasn't this done when she first moved in? How come she's had to live with these for however many horrifying weeks?' Instead I replied, 'Sure,' and followed Aunty Wynn's lead and started to move each ornament with care to the second towel- lined box on the floor.

A selection of the dolphins I handled: a pink and blue crystal-like plastic creature, leaping from a crystal-like plastic sea; a poorly painted plaster thing, probably a gift from Bethany; a set of three metal medallions, each illustrating a different species; a cheap wooden relief with 'Gold Coast Australia' burned into the bottom; a smooth wooden carving the size and shape of a hotdog. My mother was watching me with an amused expression as I reached up to the shelf and then carefully placed each ornament in the box. I could tell she was surprised by how helpful I was being—even though this was one of the tasks she had allocated to me. She knew nothing of what Aunty Wynn and I had said to each other earlier that day at the pool, or how I was trying to turn over a new leaf.

'I don't care what you all think,' Aunty Wynn said, sharing the tail end of an internal monologue. 'I just love them.'

A few seconds passed in silence. A day ago, my mother and I would have exchanged sniggers, or at the very least a raising of eyebrows or rolling of the eyes. Now I didn't look in her direction. I wanted to be a neutral player.

'Did I hear you say something about Mum's knitting?' I asked.

'Your mum used to collect knitting patterns,' Aunty Wynn

said. 'She couldn't knit. I think she just liked the pictures.' She looked at my mother, who was pretending to yawn. 'She used to stick them to her bedroom wall, this room right here.'

I hadn't known that room had been my mother's original bedroom—that explained some of why she wanted to be there now. But it wasn't that weird to me that she had collected knitting patterns in her youth. She loved knitting. She had done it all my life, until she lost the fine use of her hands. I thought of all those big chunky scarves she had knitted while watching me swim. Aunty Wynn didn't seem to know about any of that. Then I thought about how before my mother moved back here, we'd donated the last of her knitting projects— dozens of scarves, sweaters, slippers, made and lightly worn and then stashed away in cupboards over a couple of decades—to the Red Cross store in Wellington.

Maybe Aunty Wynn would have liked some of them.

'Really?' I asked now, about the knitting patterns, directing the question to my mother.

My mother shrugged. She was pretending not to be interested. She didn't want Aunty Wynn to know that she had knitted for decades and never once knitted something with her sister in mind. I imagined Aunty Wynn opening one of my mother's cupboards back home and discovering piles of knitted goods: a symbol of my mother's secret life, so removed from Aunty Wynn's.

But it wasn't even a secret life. We hadn't spent any energy keeping it from her—we'd just never thought to share it.

'When did you start collecting these?' I asked, wanting to change the subject.

'Nineteen seventy-eight,' Aunty Wynn said. She was examining a dolphin made of blue and white blown glass: the kind of object you would see in a middle-aged nurse's house. More than the strange plaster, wooden, and stone renditions I'd already handled. She lightly huffed onto it and then wiped

it with a handkerchief she had pulled from her pants pocket. It was clear this dolphin held a special significance.

'That long ago?' I said.

When she didn't say anything more, I looked to my mother. Her expression was first mocking and then faintly melancholy. She pulled at her iPad and started typing. When she was done she gestured to me.

VET

Though Aunty Wynn wouldn't have told my mother everything we'd shared in the changing room, from the teasing look on my mother's face I could tell she knew that I knew Stephen and Aunty Wynn had once been in*volved*.

So Stephen the vet had started Aunty Wynn's dolphin obsession, and the glass specimen Aunty Wynn was inspecting was the original. I tried to think of something to say that would please my mother and not hurt Aunty Wynn. But I couldn't get past the idea of a grown single woman collecting these trinkets, some of them so weird, so ugly, because they reminded her of the man she loved, a man she could not have, and who had since let her down. It depressed me, which made me think harshly of Aunty Wynn. She should burn the trinkets, I thought, or bury them. Throw them into the harbour.

When I'd filled my box, I followed Aunty Wynn into the dark and musty dining room, the least-used room in the house, where there were two new shelves placed against the far wall, so her dolphins would be mostly obscured by the large dining table and sideboard. Anyone walking into the room would see them, but they weren't exactly being given pride of place as Aunty Wynn had said—if they were, they would be in the kitchen or the living room, the rooms where people actually *lived*. I arranged the dolphins carefully though—it was the most I could think of to offer Aunty Wynn in that moment. I placed them on the shelves in a way that made sense, that showed their best sides—big ones at the back, small at the

front, similar materials and colours grouped together—my own mini curating gig.

Aunty Wynn noticed. 'You've got a good eye for arranging things.'

Maybe—I was yet to show her and my mother the photographs from Mean Space.

It was unremarkable, that time spent in my mother's old bedroom handling Aunty Wynn's dolphins, and then arranging them again in their new home. The reason I recall it is that it was the moment I realised I was in possession of real power—a power that made me feel necessary, even strong. I knew things my mother didn't know, and things Aunty Wynn didn't know—things that could hurt them. It went without saying they also knew things about me. For the first time, I felt that we were all necessary cogs in the one family machine.

If I could drive, I might have asked to borrow a car to get back to Bethany's, but I felt silly asking for a lift. Also, no one offered. So, maybe it was the couple of small drinks I'd had with dinner—Aunty Wynn had surprised me with a bottle of vodka—or maybe it was the thought of having to walk the long way around to Bethany's, or the thought of leaving my mother and Aunty Wynn when we were having a tolerable time together—whatever it was, I decided to use Aunty Wynn's map to make a shortcut across the back paddock.

I stepped down from the slick wooden steps at the back of the house, and felt the damp lawn seep through the sides of my sneakers. It was cold. The temperature had dropped since I'd last been outside, when I'd brought in the still-damp togs and towels from the line before dinner. Aunty Wynn had lent me a giant, Paddington-Bear-yellow parka that came down to my knees and had to be rolled up at the sleeves.

I eyed the rickety wire fence behind Uncle Cliff's vegetable

garden semi-circle. I rearranged my satchel and squeezed myself through the loose wires. Standing on the other side, a few steps back, I turned and observed the Moore family house. It was only just after six, but already it was nearing pitch-black out. The house looked less decrepit in the dark, the lights in the kitchen and my mother's room giving it a friendly glow. From that short distance, it looked like a place someone might want to be.

My destination was roughly two hundred metres away. I walked towards the streetlights in the direction the map suggested, while keeping the large yellow torch that Aunty Wynn had retrieved from under the kitchen sink directed at the ground in front of me. I didn't want to trip on uneven bits of paddock or large thistles.

Though I thought I knew for sure that the paddock was animal- free, I stopped and passed the torch across the horizon. First, in a half circle to my right. Nothing. A few crickets were singing in the mānuka trees, and I heard the faint *maw-pawrk* call of a lone morepork. I swung the torch to my left and behind me. That was when I saw, behind Uncle Cliff's teepee gardens, and illuminated by a square of light coming from a high back window of the sleep-out, two figures embracing.

In a fright, I switched off the torch. Though he was facing away from me, there was no doubt that one of the figures was Uncle Cliff. I recognised his slightness and how he stood with one knee bent. As my eyes adjusted to the dark, and my brain adjusted, too, I realised there wasn't a second figure. Not a human one at least. Uncle Cliff was only tending to his horse, brushing its mane with long gentle strokes.

I watched him for a while and wondered if he would take me for a ride—I'd never ridden a horse before. I breathed deeply, and I found myself feeling strangely light-hearted. Things weren't on the up—my mother was still going to die on Tuesday, and I was still helping her do it—but I had this

feeling that something was shifting positively inside of me. The shifting might be better described as a dull shimmering. A small square of light like that square of light from Uncle Cliff's sleep-out, but aimed instead at dusty carpet—now bright, now fading, now gone, now bright again as the cloudy day continues outside. That's how I felt. And I was certain I would look back on that moment as significant beyond everything that had happened, and was yet to happen.

According to Aunty Wynn's map, the fence in front of me belonged to house #11—the house across the street from Bethany's. At one corner of the #11 property the fence disappeared into the dark mānuka trees. At the other it was joined to the slightly higher fence of a neighbouring house. I decided to try a running jump and hoist myself up. I don't know how I managed it while holding the torch, but I did. And from where I was positioned, straddling #11's fence, I could see lights on inside the house: one that lit up the kitchen, another in a front room, and a small porchlight that partially illuminated the backyard. Through the branches of a tree just inside the fence I could also see what looked like a child's playhouse and half a kidney-shaped swimming pool.

The next stage of my plan went something like this: I would use a branch of that spindly tree to swing into the backyard, then I would follow the path down the left side of the house, the side without any lights on, which would hopefully take me to a front gate. It hadn't occurred to me that I would be trespassing, or that anyone might be inside the house and able to see me. So it certainly didn't occur to me that anyone would be in the backyard, and absolutely not in the swimming pool. But there was someone in the swimming pool. I could see them now as they floated into the kidney half that wasn't obscured by the branch in front of me.

It was a man and he was floating on his back. For a moment the sight confused me. I guessed the pool was heated because there was steam rising off it, but that didn't explain the cat. It took me a few more seconds to understand what I was looking at. Though I'd had only a couple of small vodkas with dinner, I felt drunk.

What I saw was a man floating on his back with his arms extended, as if nailed to a cross. There was also a cat sitting, quite calmly, on the section of the man's chest that wasn't submerged. I couldn't see the man's feet—I guessed he was using them to propel himself around the pool.

I felt a shiver up my spine. I had the vague sense of hovering above myself—watching myself watch that man, who was obviously some kind of loon, and knowing that I should get off the fence and walk back across the paddock. Then the man turned his head and looked directly at me.

'Who's up there?' he said.

I'd switched the torch back on when I'd reached the top of the fence, and I was shining it straight at him. I saw myself doing this, but I did nothing to stop.

'No one,' I said. It slipped out. Again, I felt like I was watching all of this happen from a distance.

'I can see you're someone,' the man said.

'No,' I said.

'I can see you and I can hear you. What're you doing sitting on my fence?'

'I'm not!' I cried, as I tried to slide back down the fence— the torch banging out my progression. The movement wasn't effective. Aunty Wynn's parka snagged on something, while my left leg remained hooked over the top of the fence. With difficulty I tried to pull myself back up far enough to unhook the parka, but the rubber sole of my right shoe kept slipping on the damp wooden slats, and my satchel was also getting in the way.

Then I felt the weight of a hand on my foot.

I called out. I struggled and kicked to free myself from the hand.

'You're not a kid,' the man said. His voice was deep.

I could only make out the top of his head—his hair was wet. When he spoke again I stopped kicking.

'You know,' he said, 'there's a gate in the middle of my fence.'

'What?' I said. Then, because I suddenly didn't feel like I was in any danger, which had always been my problem and would continue to be my problem for some time to come—my initial cautiousness with men quickly followed by a complete letting down of my guard, all at once and with no good rationale—I said, 'Where's the cat?'

'Pancake's right here,' the man said. He removed his hand from my foot. 'Do you need some help?'

'I need to get to my cousin's house. She's across the road.'

'The hippy girl with the stringy hair?'

'That could be Bethany,' I said. 'Our family used to own this land.'

'If you drop down I'll open the gate,' the man said. Then he was gone.

I paused for a moment, still hanging there on the fence. I thought about running back across the paddock. But I wouldn't do it. I felt completely disarmed now, which had the ill effect of also making me feel safe. I manoeuvred myself to the ground.

The man was already standing in a new space in the middle of the fence.

'I didn't know there was a gate here,' I said.

'How would you,' he said.

He was in his early thirties, weekend fit but with a noticeable paunch, his legs two thin wide-set poles holding up his dripping red and blue board shorts. I wasn't immediately attracted to him, but that beard, so full and clean, and the droplets of water that had collected at the corners of his mouth and chin

contributed something—a vulnerability, ruggedness? That was the problem with a man with a beard though, wasn't it? What did the beard stand for that the face couldn't?

'I'm Craig,' he said. His smile, what I could make out, was mocking.

'I'm Erin,' I said.

He led me down the right side of the house along a garden path faintly lit by the back-porch light and the glow from the kitchen. I could see goosebumps forming on his arms and back, which endeared him to me some. He was taller than me, though not by much. I thought I could take him down if need be.

'You lived here long?' I asked.

'Long enough,' he said. He turned to face me. 'What's up with your hair?'

I touched the side of my head. The question made me feel newly uncertain about my hair colour. 'I dyed it for a performance,' I said. 'I'm an artist.'

'What kind?'

'Performance,' I said, scoffing. The lie came out of nowhere. I looked down at my torch. I wanted to flesh out my response, but I couldn't think of anything that would require me to dye my hair grapefruit pink.

Craig didn't look convinced either. He ran his hand over his beard, in the way of every man I'd ever met who could grow a beard like that. The cat had followed us. It stood at attention between Craig's feet as Craig unlatched the gate and held it open.

'Wouldn't you just get a wig?' he said.

'Thanks for letting me use your gates,' I said.

'If you get bored while you're around,' he said, again with what could have been a mocking smile, 'you're welcome to come for a swim.'

I didn't respond. Maybe I was afraid of what I might say.

As I squeezed past Craig and his cat and out through the gate, Craig did something that both repulsed and thrilled me: he reached up and touched my hair. He didn't pull it, or stroke it, he just ran his fingers along the bottom, gently, as you might when inspecting and enjoying the shape of a newly clipped shrub.

Bethany opened the front door while I was crossing Freshfields Meadow. She looked puzzled. I wondered how much of my exchange with Craig she had seen.

'Welcome to Freshfields fucking Palace,' she said, equal parts gregarious and aggressive.

As the contents of her bedroom had suggested, in the time since last year's family get-together she had transformed from a skinny round-shouldered fifteen-year-old bogan to a big-breasted, straight-backed hippy chick. Her face was still thick with make-up but her hair was no longer bottle black—it had returned to its original mousy brown. And her clothes! She was wearing phenomenally flared jeans with floral and tartan patches on her knees and thighs. On top: a very small yellow T-shirt with John Lennon's face on it, stretched unflatteringly across her boobs and cropped to expose a gaudy bellybutton piercing. It looked like she had ironed on the John Lennon picture herself.

After a brief exchange of deadpan pleasantries—Bethany had also acquired braces, which twinkled as she spoke—she guided me to her bedroom. She had a jaunty walk—different from how I remembered. She was wearing the same socks as me, white with pink cats, though mine were damp and grubby around the toes and heel and the cats were more brown on taupe. I felt deflated being back inside that house. It was to do with all that cream and beige, the Beatles memorabilia and the lingering damp, combined with the shock of Bethany's new look.

Then I saw the teepee. I only glimpsed it through the open

kitchen doors, but it was hard to miss. The two-by-four construction I'd seen in the backyard earlier in the afternoon had since been transformed. And was that smoke I could smell?

'What do you want to do exactly?' Bethany asked, throwing herself down in the wheelie chair with force. Every part of her had grown: her torso, her arms and legs, those boobs. She was turning into a monster of a woman.

'I need to download some music,' I said. I'd taken off Aunty Wynn's giant parka, which I now folded and placed on the floor next to the torch. I took out my phone and its cord. 'And just use the internet.'

Bethany nodded while she entered her password and the computer started to load. She didn't immediately get up from the chair.

'And maybe the printer,' I said.

She pointed at the printer, implying: there it is, you can use it.

'What sort of music exactly?' she said. She might have been trying to be helpful, but she flung the question at me with vehemence.

'Some things for Mum,' I said.

The year before, Bethany had been such a pathetic kid—my little emo cousin from the small-town north. Though I found her new bolshiness curious, my desire for a sibling had long faded. She had always been Dumb Cousin Bethany, and my new warmer feelings for Aunty Wynn and Uncle Cliff hadn't yet spilled over to her.

'I've got a lot of music,' she said. 'And I mean *a lot*.'

In silence, we watched while the computer finished loading, then Bethany opened a browser. I was still waiting for her to get out of the chair. Every second she didn't I felt increasingly irritable. She was staring at the screen and making a clicking noise with her tongue against the roof of her mouth. Finally she started typing something into the search bar.

I watched her spell it out: *Craig is a fucking dick.*

'I'll show you my collection,' she said when she was done.

Aunty Wynn had given her too much rope. When I'd learned Bethany was living on her own, even though she hadn't yet finished high school, I hadn't cared enough to think much about it. Now I wondered what she really got up to in this house. I asked her what her deal was with Craig over the road. But the most she mustered was a disgusted snort. Unkindly, I assumed her dislike of him was something to do with the intensifying weed smell in her bedroom. Or the enormous teepee in the backyard.

Bethany did have a lot of music, including everything on my mother's list: Fleetwood, Lynyrd, Tom, Janis, Linda, Bonnie, Stevie, and of course Joni.

'Does she mean the Vogel's ad?' Bethany asked.

'That's what I imagine,' I said. Music has never been my strong suit.

I'd become more self-conscious about my lack of music smarts since I'd moved to Auckland. Everyone I met outside the Art History department seemed to know about music— they all played in a band, worked at a bar where bands played, or were sleeping with someone who played in a band or worked at a bar where bands played. My last download was a Joanna Newsom album, about a decade behind everyone else. I played it when people came over, though all that harp-backed yowling about boats and fruit and shellfish was mostly beyond my enjoyment. And with regard to my mother's list of requests? I was jealous that the music she wanted to listen to on her deathbed was music she shared with Bethany, and not with me.

'Does this one have any upbeat songs on it?' I asked. I'd made Bethany open one of her Joni Mitchell albums and was reading the song titles. They didn't exactly sound upbeat. 'Because

that's what I need, what my mum wants. Upbeat.'

Bethany narrowed her eyes at me: she was trying to figure out whether I was mocking her. 'I wouldn't say upbeat,' she said. 'But I would say life-affirming.'

Was this really what my mother was looking for? I felt useless. And what did this music mean to my mother? Had she listened to this stuff when she was younger? Had she danced around our kitchen to this when I wasn't home? I didn't know. And I should have known.

'I guess I'll grab all of it,' I said.

'Put it on if you want,' Bethany said. Maybe she'd seen the defeat on my face.

'No, that's fine,' I said, shaking my head.

I looked around the room while I waited for Bethany to finish setting everything up so I could sync what I needed to my phone. That's when I saw something move inside her birdcage.

'Is that a mouse?'

Now standing beside me, Bethany was twisting her T-shirt in her hands so that it rose well above her bellybutton—like a worried child might play with their hair or suck on their sleeve. 'That's Ringo,' she said, letting the T-shirt fall, her voice blooming with pleasure. 'He's my rat.'

'Why's he in a birdcage?'

'See his cinnamon head and shoulders, how they're like a hood?' Bethany said, ignoring my question.

I certainly could. 'Gross.'

She exhaled sharply in a manner that I associated with Aunty Wynn. She was unimpressed, but behind that there flickered a desperate earnestness, a disappointment with me. 'Rats are actually very social and amazingly clean,' she said. She pushed past me, her shoulders not those of a swimmer, but their own kind of impressive. 'You'd be surprised.'

▲

I spent three hours on the internet and printed out several dozen pages on the following: veterinarians and Nembutal, pentobarbital vs. phenobarbital, PEG delivery, feeding tube flush, deliverance machine, sterile vs. non-sterile pentobarbital, 100ml Nembutal (images), 50ml Valabarb and Lethabarb (images), assisting suicide NZ law, assisting suicide sentencing. I also downloaded via Bethany's iTunes something called *All the Best Irish Folk Songs*.

Although much of what I printed off was already covered in Aunty Wynn's suicide handbook, I was feeling more confident about what we needed and what I should expect Stephen the vet to hand over the next morning. I could feel myself moving into the same zone that my mother and Aunty Wynn had been in the night before. I felt increasingly cool and collected. A movie played in my mind about how the drug exchange would go the next day. I pictured it all going extremely smoothly.

As I watched the old ink-jet printer screech out my copies, I had to listen to Bethany and her boyfriend, Brent, get increasingly drunk as they moved between the kitchen and living room. My carefree youth felt far behind me. I thought I was ready to return Karl's call.

He answered after the fourth ring. 'Hello, Karl speaking.'

As soon as I heard his tone I should have hung up. I'd called his cellphone, so he would have known it was me on the other end calling to return the message *he* had left on my phone, yet he spoke like someone receiving an anonymous business call.

'It's me,' I said. 'Erin.'

'What's up?'

'I'm returning your call,' I said. I was trying not to sound angry or nervous.

'Oh right, of course.' He turned away from the phone and said something indecipherable to the room. There was a long pause. 'How's your mum?'

I tried not to dwell on the picture of Karl standing in the same room as his wife with one or more of his children playing nearby. I guessed he would go into the hallway then maybe another room for privacy. I hadn't expected him to ask about my mother. Karl knew I was visiting her, and that she was sick, but that was all. I hadn't shared any of the finer details with him, but that wasn't what bothered me—it was the realisation that soon, in only a few days, no one would have reason to ask me that question again.

'You there?' Karl asked. Then, maybe suspecting I was putting on a sulk, he sighed self-importantly. 'This is why I think it would be best if you finished up at Mean Space early.'

That, I guess, had been the purpose of his original message. It wasn't a surprise, but his big reveal gave me reason to be freshly outraged, to dig deep for self-pity. I felt like a foolish little girl, and I channelled that energy by swearing and then flipping him the most savage middle finger I could muster down the phone.

'Openings are out of bounds for now too,' he said.

'I suppose I'm not even allowed to de-install my own show,' I said.

'No, you can do that.'

I thought I heard a tap being turned on full. 'Are you in the bathroom?' I asked. 'Was that a toilet being flushed?'

'Look, Erin,' he replied sweetly, and as with his earlier message, it sounded like he was enjoying himself. He knew I wouldn't fight this or make any trouble for him. 'I'm sorry, but you need to be mature about this.'

'You're not sorry,' I said. My voice shook. With the hand that wasn't gripping my phone, I began vigorously combing my hair back from my face.

'I *am* sorry,' he said.

'I'm sorry you're stuck with a wife with such monstrous eyes,' I said, still violently combing at my hair.

'What?' Karl said.

'You heard me.' I stood up straighter, eyed my reflection in the bedroom window. I was drunk on the adrenalin of reliving this humiliation. 'Christ, Karl,' I said. 'You can see half of her eyeballs even when her eyes are closed.'

This ridiculous comment was grounded in fact. Karl's wife did have weirdly large eyes—they were incredible—and according to Karl her eyelids didn't fully cover them when she slept. Thinking about it now, I don't believe he ever meant to tell me something so personal about his wife. It had just slipped out. But at the time—post- coital, slumped on the floor of the gallery storage room—I'd thought that Karl had wanted to tell me, and that he had done so because he didn't love her. So I'd convinced myself that this *flaw* was some kind of deal-breaker for him, and a sign I had a chance. At the tail end of this disastrous phone conversation, though, it was just a silly, petty thing that popped into my head, and further proof that I was the fool on the line.

After that, Karl hung up.

I went to the kitchen for a glass of water. While I was running the tap, Bethany appeared from outside and began mixing herself a large rum and Coke. The French doors were hooked open despite the night's cool temperature. Brent, whom I still hadn't met, was sitting outside on one of the lawn-chairs—I could see the top of his head though the rest of him was in shadow. Now that I was closer I could see smoke pouring from the entrance and top of the teepee.

'Brent worships the cold,' Bethany said. Her voice was an Aunty Wynn kind of boom, but unsteady, drunk. Her

tone revealed nothing about how much she had heard of my conversation with Karl, and she seemed over our earlier exchange about her pet rat. Her ability to brush things off was something she had got from her mother. I envied her for it.

There were several bottles of bottom-shelf liquor arranged in a line on the kitchen counter. Despite how defeated I felt, I didn't want any of it. Though I couldn't see a stereo, I could hear Neil Young singing, 'Are you ready for the country?' Holding my glass of water with two hands, I walked to the French doors and looked out. I'd already put Aunty Wynn's parka back on to prepare myself for the walk back to the Moore family house. Bethany stood beside me and slurped her drink. The ice rolled and chinked against her braces.

'That's my boyfriend,' she said. 'He likes to lie out there and look for Orion.'

I was more interested in the teepee. Several large blue tarpaulins had been wrapped around the wooden frame and tied down with yellow rope and elastic bungee cords. It was both impressive and a badly constructed totem of bad vibes.

'Is the fire okay?' I asked. The smoke was thick and swirling grey, pink, and stale orange. A house fire felt like a terrifyingly appropriate finale to the last two days.

'The wood's just a bit wet,' Bethany said. 'It was lying outside at the vet's—they were clearing out some stuff. I've been working there once a fortnight.'

That segue was a classic Aunty Wynn move. In the last year, Bethany had acquired a lot more of Aunty Wynn's approaches to conversation. Namely, she didn't need it to be a two-way street, and she didn't like silences. I let her talk. Already, I wanted to try Karl again. 'Mostly I just take out the trash and clean stuff for Steve,' she was saying.

I hadn't forgotten Aunty Wynn's comments in the kitchen the day before about Bethany wanting to go to vet school. As I'd since learned a thing or two about Stephen the vet, it horrified

me to think that Aunty Wynn might have had to ask that man for another favour. Bethany had no idea about any of it—the way she cheerfully called him Steve was the giveaway. I could fill in the gaps for her, knock her down a few pegs.

'I'm really there to, you know, soak it all up,' she said. 'I want to work with zoo animals. Something cute like pygmy marmosets.' She giggled.

I was reminded she was only going on seventeen. She didn't have a clue. She started picking at something in her braces as Brent crossed the lawn and entered the teepee. Smoke was still rising from its top. I imagined the two of them sitting inside and a light wind surprising them, then the structure falling and the two of them trapped. Not a house fire, but I could see it happening. And, once I left, I wouldn't be able to hear their calls for help. Would Craig hear them? Or Lia down the street?

'The smoke's worse because we're burning porn mags,' Bethany said, deadpan as she could handle. It was clear from the lilt in her voice how much she delighted in saying this out loud. 'The pages are pretty plasticky.' Whatever she had been digging around for in her braces had been extracted, swallowed.

'Just watch you don't kill yourself,' I said. As I said it, something pulled taut in my chest, like a knot of rope being tightened against the trunk of a tree.

'Oh yeah,' Bethany said, skiing in her socks across the lino to the kitchen counter. Her arms swung by her sides like a wasted ice-skater's. 'There's nothing to play music on back at the house. You'll need this.'

From behind the bottles of booze, she retrieved a small black and white figurine. She yanked a plug from the wall and the music abruptly stopped. 'I've got a better one in my room,' she said, as she handed the Bluetooth speaker to me with a drunk but sincere smile. I thought I saw her looking longingly at my hair.

The speaker was in the shape of a panda bear, and very cheap-

looking—the kind of system you could buy from a display by the checkout line at the supermarket: This week only! $24.99, etc. I'll admit it was thoughtful of Bethany to anticipate my need for it, but already I was imagining how I would set it up in my mother's room, how I would play from my phone one of the albums from Bethany's collection, and how my mother, Aunty Wynn, and I would try and avoid the panda's expressionless eyes while we listened to a supermarket-quality Joni Mitchell singing one of her melancholic songs. And then what? Would Aunty Wynn and I watch my mother shakily drug herself? I didn't believe that was the kind of *final frolic* my mother was hoping for. But what more could I do to make it any less shitty?

Ever since the previous afternoon, when in the paddock with the stuck goat Aunty Wynn had told me about my mother's plans, my feelings were constantly changing. I couldn't settle myself and I was exhausted. But I felt like I'd been holding it together. Like a well-spun top, I was keeping my centre of gravity—just. Now, looking at that Bluetooth speaker made me feel that I wouldn't make it through the next couple of days after all. My spinning top had the speed wobbles. If I didn't simply crash, I felt as if the force of my spinning might suddenly make me airborne and send me flying headfirst through the roof of Bethany's kitchen.

So this is what I did next: I placed the speaker in my satchel, with the torch, all of the printed material, and the last third of the bag of Twisties, which made a loud crinkling sound that Bethany could, by the look on her face, definitely hear. Then I crossed Freshfields Meadow and knocked on Craig's front door.

6

Craig answered the door wearing a pink and green towel that covered him from his bellybutton to his shins.

'And here you are,' he said.

We moved silently around each other as though it were perfectly normal that I should be returning to his house at such an hour. When he reached behind me to close the front door, again his hand brushed against my hair, this time grazing my earlobe. I shuddered— both from the cold and the pleasure of his touch. I edged off my shoes.

Standing in his kitchen I eyed his backyard from a new angle: the tree by the high wooden fence, the child's playhouse, or was it a doghouse, the swimming pool undisturbed and glassy. At the mercy of that porchlight—all long shadows, muted colours—the backyard looked like the set of some creepy TV show.

Though nothing had happened yet, I was already annoyed by the guilt that I felt for being there, for standing in that kitchen. The feeling deepened as I tuned into the music coming from Craig's living room: growling heavy metal. And there was a fishy smell—Craig's cat was crouched on the far end of the kitchen counter, noisily eating from a can of tuna that had been set down on a floral placemat. Only then was I able to admit to myself what I hadn't wanted to admit while crossing the road and before knocking on Craig's door—I was about to make a mistake.

I placed my satchel on the counter, at the opposite end from the cat.

'I suppose you want a drink,' Craig said.

I tried not to stare at his bare torso. I thought about what I'd seen earlier: Craig gliding around the pool on his back with that cat curled up on his chest. I wanted to know what he had been doing, but I couldn't find the words to ask. There was something uneasy about the man, and I was remembering how I'd first hooked up with Karl— on the back of another breakup. I didn't trust myself to do this properly, to not get myself into a mess.

'My cousin has been plying me with booze all night,' I said, though it wasn't true. I could see flakes of dried tuna, remnants from this meal and previous ones, fanning out from the cat's can and onto its placemat and the surrounding countertop. I felt nauseated. 'So, no drink for me. I'm good.'

Craig had already retrieved two glasses and a bottle of Jameson.

'Your cousin's a bit of a booze hag,' he said.

It alarmed me to hear him talk about Bethany like that— Bethany, my clueless teenage cousin. But rather than coming to her defence or asking him to explain what he meant, or listening to the alarm bells going off and getting the hell out of there, I got jealous, and I rushed to outdo her.

'My mother has motor neurone disease,' I said. I felt disgusted with myself for telling him, but what I said next was worse. 'She'll probably be dead in a couple of months, but she wants to die on Tuesday.'

I hadn't planned on telling him anything about myself. The information had come out of its own volition. Again I felt drunk, even though the effect of the vodka with dinner had long since worn off.

Craig was looking at me with his head cocked to the side like a curious spaniel, frowning. 'I don't know what that is,' he said. As he eyed me, he started to absently twirl his fingers in the butt of his beard.

Surely I had nothing to worry about. What could this man

possibly guess about what my mother and Aunty Wynn had planned? But I knew I'd made a mistake even mentioning my mother. I could feel myself unravelling, and Craig's kitchen was not the right place for it to happen. At the same time, it felt sneakily good to confess those things out loud.

'It's no big deal,' I said, back-tracking.

Craig slid a full glass of whiskey across the counter. I picked it up but didn't drink. Craig took a wide gulp from his. We watched each other. I placed my glass back down. Then Craig was standing in front of me and pushing off Aunty Wynn's parka. He peeled back my cardigan, lifted off my T-shirt. Already my jeans were folded down to my knees. Though when I reached for Craig's towel he shied away.

'Let's go sit on the couch,' he said.

As I was tugging off my jeans, I thought: I could be halfway back to the house by now. Despite how quickly Craig and I had reached this point, and how much I wanted to forget Karl, to have something new for myself, I wasn't exactly eager to be here. So why did I stay?

Not long before Karl, there was a guy I'd slept with intensely for a couple of months. His beard was similar in its fullness to Craig's— long and thick, with only the thinnest indication of a bottom lip. One night I'd shown up at the guy's apartment and a completely different figure answered the door. The guy had, for whatever reason, shaved off that beard. At first I gasped. Then I started to laugh—the kind of laughter that comes from being ill at ease. His face was completely naked. It was disconcerting to look at. I would have been less shocked if he had answered the door actually naked. His face made me think of a once impressive longhaired cat, maybe a Maine Coon or Persian, after a big chunk had been shaved out of it at the vet's. Reduced. I'd come to view that guy's full beard as his true face, so who was I now looking at?

The guy forgave me for my reaction, but after that I quickly

lost interest in him. I didn't like the new version. The smooth openness of that face made me feel as though I might end up getting to know him more intimately than I wanted. I'd appreciated that beard for the screen it provided between us. My attraction to Craig was equally simplistic, shallow. I had no intention of getting to know him beyond whatever happened that night. I only wanted sex—a base comfort, a distraction.

Loneliness had been one of the few consistencies in my life for the past year and a bit. It was a gaping, untouchable kind of loneliness that I'd never previously experienced.

Craig was watching me over the rim of his glass of whiskey. I left my jeans in a heap on the kitchen floor and followed him into the warm living room. The backside of his towel revealed the interlaced necks of two pink flamingos, their eyes red hearts, and in the background a plump green sea.

'What do you want to listen to?' he said, scanning his CD rack, something I hadn't seen in a while. 'I know, something mellow.'

From where I was standing I could see too many CD covers with flames, skulls and Gothic fonts to be confident about his definition of 'mellow'. He took off the metal CD and put on some Queen, turning the volume down so it was a background operatic rumble.

'That's better,' he said, nodding along to his selection.

Craig's house had the same layout as Bethany's but flipped on its head. In the living room there was the same overwhelming onslaught of beige: carpet, walls and curtains. Only two things stuck out: 1) the couch, which was made of white faux-leather—a porn star's couch, and 2) that the rest of the room's beige theme was broken up by a collection of hideous paintings and one painting that very much wasn't hideous. It was hanging on the wall opposite the white couch, unframed, no bigger than a tea towel. I took a few steps closer, looked at it properly.

'What's this?' I said.

'That?' Craig frowned at the painting as if seeing it for the first time. 'It belonged to my aunt,' he said. 'I think she might've painted it even.'

From a distance the painting looked purposefully sad and disgusting, a lot of thick browns and greys, like a vulgar abstraction of a table laid with a Sunday roast. Up close the colour combinations and the brushstrokes were exciting, though—that grey-brown next to that hot pink and lemon yellow! I didn't know who Craig's aunt was, but I knew that painting didn't belong on that wall. It was surrounded by three impressively awful examples of paint applied to canvas: a badly executed jug of sunflowers à la van Gogh, four cartoonish cows dancing the grapevine on their hind legs, and a triptych of psychedelic koru-like swirls and waves. I assumed they had all been made by a group of individuals on day release at some kind of community arts and crafts centre and picked up by Craig for five bucks apiece at the local Red Cross.

'So what's this other crap doing on the walls?' I asked.

'What do you mean?'

'If you don't know what I mean, then I can't help you,' I said. I sat down on the couch and snorted arrogantly.

'You like it?' Craig said, nodding at his aunt's painting. I got the sense he was looking forward to my approval.

When I didn't immediately reply, he looked eagerly in the direction of the painting with the dancing cows. 'Those cows are classic,' he said. And then, more seriously, looking towards the two- metre wide triptych of bright orange, yellow, green— hell, all the colours of the rainbow—whirlpools and ripples: 'I got a woman I know to make that three-piece one for me.'

The triptych was too detailed and steady to have been produced by a child, though the individual panels looked strikingly similar to some pastel and dye inspirations I'd created

in primary school. One swirl in the middle panel, which had been painted in a flesh-like peach, looked remarkably, disturbingly, like a foetus. I turned away from it.

I'd always looked on certain failures without forgiveness. For as long as I could remember, I hated the sight of a man swimming who could not swim well: flailing arms, legs both sinking and breaking the surface of the water in large wild kicks, gaping mouth, a mild look of panic on his face. How many men I'd seen attack the water like that, and then confidently emerge from the pool like they had done it right. How could they not see themselves? How could I trust them in any other arena of their lives? Similarly, how could Craig not see himself now? I looked at his pale chest rising and falling as he looked from the intense and sad little gem of a painting to the three-part monstrosity.

Whatever intensity had passed between us in his backyard and kitchen was beginning to subside. The small determination I'd felt to see this through was waning. I looked at him, half-heartedly daring him to sit next to me, or remove his towel, or something.

'You think you're pretty special, don't you?' he said. He wasn't smiling.

I shrugged. I might have been smirking. Craig wasn't the first guy to ask that sort of question. At the right time, usually when I'd been drinking, though I was perfectly sober now, I had a way of sitting, speaking, moving around men that could rile them up. Or turn them on. I couldn't tell what Craig was thinking—whether he wanted me or wanted to hit me.

Then something passed across his face that made me think the latter. For a moment I felt uneasy. And very naked, sitting on that ridiculous faux-leather couch in only my undies, bra, and muddy cat socks. I shrugged again, more apologetically this time. Craig's expression didn't change, but as I went to

get up, he moved towards me so his legs were touching mine, blocking me, then he shifted his weight so his knees were pinning mine into the couch.

I had an uncertain, creeping bad feeling about what was to follow. I sat motionless, kept my eyes on his. At the same time, the heat pump mounted on the living room wall behind me whirred into action, blowing hot air onto my shoulders and neck. The heat pump was loud, even with the music, and it had the effect of another person walking into the room. Craig's expression became warmer, the darkness in his face gone.

'You're a weird one,' he said, flopping down on my left, the couch expelling a loud farting noise as he did. He parked his right hand on my knee. 'The performance art stuff makes sense.'

I was about to object, then I remembered what I'd said to him earlier. He gripped my knee harder. His hands were large and strong. He had calluses on his palm, but his fingernails were clean, impressively attended to.

'I'm a builder,' he said. 'In case you were wondering.'

I hadn't been wondering. 'What's with this couch?' I asked.

'What do you mean?'

I can't emphasise enough how horrible that couch was to sit on— I was already sweating on the back of my thighs and behind my knees. Whenever I moved the cushions made a wretched plasticky sound.

'It's pretty off-putting,' I said.

Craig looked defeated then, which made me feel better. He stood up, walked across the room and turned up the stereo. When he returned to sit beside me, he put his hand back on my knee. A new song clicked over: 'Don't Stop Me Now'. I knew that song because the summer when I was fifteen everyone at my swimming club had been into Queen and I'd wanted to be into Queen too.

'You have very wide shoulders,' Craig said.

'I do,' I said.

'They're quite nice,' he said. And then, before I could respond, 'This would be up there with my favourite songs of all time.' He started to sing-hum along, shyly at first, then he turned to face me and shimmied in a not very convincing mime of Freddie Mercury. He was trying to be funny, to be a goof, but there was a sincerity to the way he moved. There was a part of him that hoped I was impressed.

'I'm a shooting star … I'm a racing car,' he whisper-sang, until he reached his goal: 'I wanna make a supersonic *woman* outta you!'

At which point, and without allowing me any time to object, he dived in for the pash.

Initially I'd thought it must have been the first time he'd pulled out that routine. Then I thought, No, he's done it before. The whole performance made me feel a little revolted, but not enough to stop. That feeling was also followed by a faint wave of nostalgia, something I'd forgotten—maybe *repressed* was a better word—that came cruising back as I pulled Craig closer, while he planted his tongue in my mouth and awkwardly slid the hand that was on my knee down the front of my undies.

The year that everyone was into Queen, swimming camp was held at a remote school on the east coast. (Was the Queen obsession something to do with *Wayne's World*? Was it just something that happened with teenagers? Were a fresh group of mid-teens going through the exact same obsession right now? Did Bethany love Queen too?) We trained in the school pool and slept in the classrooms, which were organised as follows: older girls, older guys, younger girls, younger guys. It was evening—the low-hanging sun was visible through the classroom windows where the older guys slept. We were hanging out, and the older girls (though none of us were older than fifteen) and the older guys (the oldest was nineteen) were on the PlayStation. I was sketching in my notebook, as back then I still had dreams of going to art school. But then, and

it happened so quietly and quickly, I remember looking up from my sketchbook to find I was the only girl left in the room. 'Bohemian Rhapsody' had been cranked up and each of the guys had retreated to his mattress, his teenaged hand moving rapidly beneath his sleeping bag, each rustling rhythmically as he worked, grunted: a small operatic chamber group of masturbation sounds.

And now, cutting through the sweet sounds of Freddie Mercury having a good time and the whirr of the heat pump behind us, I could hear Craig's breathing rate increasing, and I could see his dick had risen to form out of his flamingo towel a convincing green and pink tent. I scooted around in my seat—the couch squeaking its disapproval—to face him, but his hand, nestled firmly and flat against my pubic bone, like some kind of perverse seatbelt, held me fast to the couch.

'No,' he said. 'This is fine.'

Another time I would have come out and said, 'Are we going to have sex or what?' I didn't—because the situation was increasingly weird beyond my experience, and I was exhausted and ready to give up. And because a whole bunch of other thoughts had taken over, including how much I'd screwed up with Karl, my having to quit Mean Space, and the drug exchange with Stephen the vet early the next morning. Then my mother's face appeared in my head. I felt on the verge of an uncontrollable fit of laughter.

Craig slipped his free hand beneath his towel while his gaze moved from my breasts to my legs, then to the wide middle distance directly in front of him, which is where it stayed. Now his strong builder's hand was pumping away beneath those two flamingos, while his other hand twitched nervously beneath the elastic of my undies in such a way that would have been frustrating, had my attention not already cooled.

I had no idea what Craig wanted from me. I sat with my arms folded limply across my stomach and watched his slack-

jawed profile for a while, before I returned to looking at the small painting across the room.

I hadn't left the classroom immediately those eleven or so years ago either. It said something about my naïveté that I was the only older girl who didn't know about the older guys' group masturbation schedule. Though I'd been embarrassed, even frightened, to discover I was the only girl in that room, ringed by ten grunting teenage boys, I was also excited, turned on by what I could see. The confidence was amazing to me—how unashamedly those guys went for it. Although I left eventually, before I did I caught the eye of one of the older guys, whose buzzed head was poking out from beneath his sleeping bag. His mouth was open. His gaze focused on an imagined distance, then on me. Rather than flinching and leaving the room in a rush, I returned his gaze. And I became increasingly aware of how much my being there pleased him, how much power I had by just bearing witness.

How many times had I left a strange man's house straight after the deed and transported myself home late at night only to wake up the next morning to find I wasn't in my own bed at all? I'd only dreamt the journey. Each step so vivid it was shocking to learn I'd only walked away in my head. And again, despite what my dreams had tried to sell me, rather than waking up in Bethany's old bedroom as expected, I woke stretched out on Craig's white couch, with Craig's cat curled up in a ball on the other end, in a quiet, dark house.

I hadn't meant to fall asleep.

I'd meant to get dressed and walk back to the Moore family house.

Now the microwave clock in the kitchen read seven-thirty. I'd slept long, too long—Aunty Wynn and I were supposed to be meeting Stephen the vet soon. Though Craig had placed

a blanket over me, I was cold wearing only my underwear and socks. And the sliding door in the kitchen had been left ajar—for the cat, I guessed—letting in all the chilly morning air. Hurriedly I dressed and sculled a large glass of water. I was ready to leave but I didn't have my satchel. It wasn't in the kitchen where I thought I'd left it, so I shuffled back into the living room. There it was on the couch. Even with the lights out, I could see the faint outline of the painting by Craig's aunt. I felt sorry for it, as if it were a living thing—having to be in that house with that man, molested by those other abominations on the walls facing it.

I felt sorry for it, as I felt sorry for myself.

Then I was hit by a wave of panic, as if realising for the first time where I was and what I'd done. Today was the day we were getting the drugs for my mother. Aunty Wynn would be waiting for me now. Or, worse, she might have left without me. The idea of that was suddenly very real. I couldn't move from my spot in the centre of the living room. I felt stuck. I felt I could scream, or punch something. I could punch that cat, though maybe a neat hole in Craig's living room wall would do. Instead, I quietly, shakily unhooked the little painting.

With my satchel on one shoulder, I held the painting out in front of me, its face pitched to the sky. The colours were different in the natural morning light—more muted, humble. The distance across the paddock was shorter and less worrying in that light too. I walked briskly. A few birds were up and making a racket in the mānuka trees, otherwise, all I could hear was the sound of my own breathing and the damp slippery sound of my shoes on the dew-heavy grass. Not once did I stop and turn and take a step back towards Craig's place, or ask myself what I was doing. I felt dead calm. Like that deep, dark lake again: where things, eels, probably, but also unnameable invisible things,

brush against your legs while you're swimming. And when you're treading water, just trying to keep your head above the surface.

I was almost at the house when I saw Uncle Cliff.

He was sitting on his horse and staring away from me, towards the eastern horizon and the rising sun. The image was like something out of an old western with a backdrop of that gentle sunrise—growing from a pale kōwhai to peach to a thin wet blue. As I approached, I thought about how someone could find Uncle Cliff handsome—so straight in his saddle, his frame small but taut and strong, his face warm and open as he wriggled around to greet me.

'You're up early,' he said. 'What's that you've got there?'

I let the painting drop to my side, as I used my other hand to shade my eyes against the glare of the sun.

'Just a painting,' I said. 'A gift.'

'Go on,' he said. 'Let's see it.'

I turned the painting towards him. His expression darkened over and he nervously fingered his spectacles, which were still hanging on their fluorescent-yellow cord.

'I recognise that,' he said.

'Yeah?' I said. My stomach cartwheeled.

He sighed the deep worried sigh of someone who could clearly see the shit about to hit the fan in a spectacular fashion.

'And I don't believe,' he said, 'that the man who owned it would give anyone anything for free.'

The Monday Before

1

My father never lived with us. At the time of these events it had been three years since we had seen each other. The last time was when we'd had dinner with his wife at their Auckland home. The house was a stark, multi-levelled affair, with an infinity pool outside the downstairs living room, an elementary wine cellar, and low, wide furniture—the kind of house I might have dreamed of owning if my father hadn't got there first. That night, the pool was crammed full of his young kids' inflatable toys, though the kids were elsewhere. The three of us politely drank and ate, then as I was leaving my father handed me an envelope containing a thousand bucks in crisp fifty- dollar notes. 'I remember what it was like being your age,' he said. 'Take your friends out to dinner or buy yourself a nice coat.'

He didn't learn of my mother's illness until after her death—I didn't tell him until then. That same conversation was the first time he learned that I'd been living in Auckland, too, that I had in fact moved there less than a year after the dinner at his house. I never missed him or wished we were closer. For better or worse, my mother had always been enough. I don't believe my mother always felt the same about me. Of course, it was a different relationship for her—being the mother versus being the child—but I think that, beneath all of her charisma and bravado and constant busyness, she was lonely. She wanted more than she had got.

The closest she made it to love, at least during my life—since that wasn't what had happened with her and my father; they

had been high school sweethearts but conceived me years after—was when I was thirteen. It was with a tall and smiling guy who managed an art supplies store that neighboured the store where my mother bought her wool and knitting needles. He just started waving at her one day. John the art store guy. Besides selling pre-made canvases to art school students, he liked to go to the gym and eat a diet high in lean protein. After a few weeks of seeing John, my mother started going to the gym and cooking us high-protein meals too. She also branched out from knitting and took up watercolour painting. It was a cliché, for sure, but that's how it is, isn't it? There's nothing unusual about how easily we bend ourselves into someone slightly different to make another person like us more. And if you had asked my mother about it at the time she would have said that she wasn't changing herself for that man, she was simply expanding her horizons.

The relationship with John lasted about four months. Only once did he spend more than the five minutes at our house that it took to collect my mother for a fitness class, the movies, or an opening at what I now imagine must have been some painfully provincial art gallery. The time John did stay for dinner was my mother's only attempt to see how he might fit into our lives longer term. She baked fish.

She was a perfectly good cook, and she had made me pull my weight in the kitchen from a young age. I remember looking at the three large flounders stacked one on top of the other in a trap of greaseproof paper and newspaper, and watching as my mother gently carried them to an oven tray lined with three separate sheets of tinfoil.

'They're big,' I said.

'But thin,' my mother said. She lifted one up by its tail and twisted it from side to side so I could see what I had already seen, which was that the flounder was three-dimensional but

very flat through its middle. She placed it back on the tray and started drizzling each fish with oil.

'Aren't you going to take their heads off?' I asked.

My mother shook her head. 'Nope. This is how the dish goes.'

'I don't want to deal with the head.'

'You can eat around it,' she said. Nothing in her tone gave anything away about how nervous she might be, or how much she was hoping this dinner with John would go well. She was cool and calm, now adding capers and garlic, and nestling the lemon wedges I'd prepared around the flounders' little fins.

'I don't want it looking at me while I eat it,' I said.

My mother closed each fish into its tinfoil cocoon and slid the tray into the oven. 'It won't be looking at you,' she said matter-of-factly. 'It wishes.'

After she plated up, my mother insisted that I deliver each plate while she and John watched, sipped their drinks. She sounded panicked, bolting out of the kitchen to take her place at the table with John. I still can't figure out if this was because she was exceedingly proud of her dish or exceedingly worried.

I delivered the meals, then took my seat at the table. Each of us had a flounder nearly the circumference of the plate, the gaps around each fish filled in with florets of broccoli and a gritty rice substitute that I now know was quinoa. Each serving looked like a child's reconstruction of an underwater scene: broccoli as seaweed, quinoa as sand, and the flounder, eye sockets wide and empty, its mouth slightly parted, swimming through the middle in shock.

'Wow,' John said, as he dipped in for a deep whiff.

I liked John. He knew how to talk to me, often addressing me by my full name—'How were your splits this week, Erin Moore?'—which made me feel like a real, full person, and the

new habits that my mother had acquired since meeting him (the protein, the watercolouring) didn't—wouldn't—have a lasting impact on my life. Ultimately, I would have said that John was a really nice though somewhat unremarkable man. And that, I think, was the real problem, and why my mother was the one to end it.

She was the first to tackle the flounder. I watched her peel back the skin with her knife. John began with a tentative scoop of quinoa before following my mother's lead. I didn't touch anything. Generally speaking I wasn't a picky eater, but—that fish. Those baked-out eyes, that leathery-looking tail.

My mother and John started discussing a recent car and bicycle accident that was in the news. It had happened only five minutes from our house. The Volvo had hit the cyclist so hard that the cyclist landed twenty feet down the road and one of his legs snapped clean through.

'It's so awful,' John said. He was shaking his head. 'The poor fellow.'

'Some of those cyclists get pretty wild out there,' my mother said. 'Sometimes they just come out of nowhere.'

'There *are* a lot of blind corners in this city,' John said.

'They said he would eventually walk fine,' my mother said definitively.

I interrupted with a snort of disgust, in the way only a thirteen- year-old girl can. I pushed my plate into the middle of the table.

'I can't eat this,' I said.

Without looking in my direction my mother said, 'Yes, you can,' and she leaned across the table and pushed the plate back in front of me, exactly as if I were a toddler. 'He'll probably be back on the road in no time,' she said to John.

John went to speak, but I got in first. 'I'm not eating it,' I said, snorting again.

'Erin, you're being juvenile,' my mother said plainly. 'It's not very appealing.'

She didn't get embarrassed easily, and she wasn't moved by my display. I should have backed down and just eaten the fish. I should have made an effort for her sake. Instead I laughed a determined little laugh.

Now John made his move.

'It tastes pretty delicious, Erin,' he said carefully, and with too much emphasis on *pretty*. Though it may have been for my benefit, it came off as a slight towards my mother.

I smirked at that. My mother ignored John entirely. And that was the moment everyone at the table knew that John had no chance with us. He should have got up and left right then.

When he took my mother out, he always dressed the same: in straight-legged jeans, button-down shirt, merino sweater, and high-shine leather dress shoes. It was the kind of nice formal-casual outfit you might wear to the wedding of a cousin you had lukewarm feelings about. That was how he had shown up to our house on that Saturday evening. My mother was wearing her standard home clothes: jazzy tights, a man's old business shirt, oversized sweatshirt, socks. I was wearing the same tracksuit bottom and T- shirt I'd worn to swimming training that morning and bummed around the house in all day. My hair was tied back in a bun that still hadn't properly dried. I probably stank of chlorine. In summary: neither of us had made any effort with our appearance. Throughout, John remained the outsider and we didn't create a space for him to properly enter our circle of two.

'This is exactly what I was talking about,' my mother said, picking up an argument we'd been having a couple of days earlier.

'I don't know what you're talking about,' I said, feigning innocence.

'You think you can do what you want,' she said. 'That you can

have whatever you want, however you want it.'

This was how things went with us—the quick escalation, both of us digging in our heels. It could happen at any time.

During this exchange, I'd been staring at the tabletop above my plate, and not looking my mother in the eye—not looking that fish in the eye sockets! Now I did look at my mother. I stared her down. 'This is so weird,' I said. I pointed at the fish in front of me. Then I pointed at her fish, and then at John's fish.

This was what my mother did next: she picked up her knife and stabbed my fish between its eye sockets. Then she picked up her fork and began peeling back the skin and the flesh, then she held that fork loaded with fish in front of my mouth.

'Eat it,' she said.

Her hand, a few inches from my face—I can still see it. So unashamed. So steady.

'Seriously, Mum?'

She moved the fork so it was pressing into my lips.

I took the bite. I couldn't see another way out. I made a scene out of dragging my teeth across the fork—my last attempt at an upper hand.

When I'd cleared the fork, my mother smiled politely. Then she removed her knife from my fish and proceeded to work away at her own flounder. After that, the dinner more or less moved forward as normal: small talk, scraping of utensils, my mother and I not saying anything about what had happened, and neither of us acting as if we felt apologetic or self-conscious.

I realise now how weird we must have seemed. I'm not sure what kind of excuse one might concoct to explain away my mother's response, though from the outside it must have looked like I was a teenager rebelling, a daughter not wanting this strange man to take her mother away. Maybe I was acting up or showing off a little— when my mother stopped seeing John I did feel partly responsible— but that wasn't all of it. We were too used to having only the other around. Our space was small,

hermetically sealed, only for two. It was suffocating sometimes, for sure, but it was what it was. I honestly believe that for a moment during that dinner, we had both simply forgotten we had a guest. Neither of us were performing differently from how we usually did. This was just how we worked.

Even though John might have been good for my mother—a quiet, balancing shadow to her bright colours and bolshiness—she always wanted more. She always wanted bigger and better. This had made it hard for her to settle down with that nice bloke, or any other. She would never have settled for the kind of relationship Aunty Wynn had had with Stephen the vet, though I wasn't sure that she wouldn't have been extremely jealous of it anyway. But it was all of her determination, her ambition and wanting, that made it possible for her to leave the Moore family farm straight out of high school, put herself through university, go to live in London, then buy a house in Wellington and raise me, all on her own.

It was the same stuff that gave her the guts to finish her life the way she wanted, too.

2

'He brought Jessica,' Aunty Wynn said.

'Who?'

It was nearly nine in the morning on Queen's Birthday Monday. There was one other vehicle in the parking lot of the local butcher's shop—a dark red farm truck. Its driver stared at us out of his closed window as we pulled up alongside, leaving a parking spot between our vehicle and theirs. That was my first glimpse of Stephen the vet. We were late.

'Who's Jessica?' I asked again.

I couldn't see anyone else in the truck. My idea of how that morning would go did not include a fourth person. The uncomfortable sleep on Craig's couch and the slow dawning of what I had done, the unnecessary trouble I might have brought on myself and the rest of the family by stealing that painting, was making me equal parts jumpy and sapped. It was made worse by the bouquet of smells in Aunty Wynn's car—chlorine, air freshener, a faint vomit smell still lingering from Saturday. I'd generously cracked the window, though it had done little to help.

Aunty Wynn's hand hovered over her seatbelt buckle. She didn't seem able to commit to undoing it.

'This is the right thing to do, isn't it?' She didn't look at me when she spoke.

I was surprised to hear her say this, and so close to the finish line. Surprised and annoyed. And hungry. After speaking with Uncle Cliff in the paddock, I'd only had time to stash the painting in Bethany's old bedroom cupboard before Aunty Wynn and I were on the road.

'Yes,' I said, reaching over to press the seatbelt buckle for her. The belt whizzed back. She still didn't move.

'Jessica's in the back seat,' she said.

I craned my neck so I could see into the truck. That's when I saw the golden muzzle fogging up a rear window—Stephen the vet had brought his Labrador.

If a dog was the only witness Stephen could rope in, I figured we would get through this. 'Let's go,' I said.

Then Stephen the vet and I were facing each other.

He was tall and surprisingly handsome. Dressed in clean blue jeans, a red Swanndri zipped up over an ironed blue button-down, he looked like a man modelling a country vet for an EziBuy catalogue. His face was pocked with acne scars which, coupled with those two dimples, one in each cheek, made him appear instantly trustworthy and much younger than his nearly sixty years. He offered me his hand. He was trying not to look at Aunty Wynn as she walked around the car to join us.

'You must be Erin,' he said.

I don't know why, but until that moment I'd thought I would remain anonymous throughout the meeting.

'Stephen the vet?' I asked, shaking his hand.

He nodded, his dimples retreating deeper. This was the man who, while in his early twenties, had gone into a gift shop or a jeweller's or whatever kind of store sold glass ornaments in the late 1970s and had chosen that special blown-glass dolphin with Aunty Wynn on his mind. Maybe he had been thinking of her as my mother had described her to me: moving through the water as effortlessly as a goddamn dolphin. Or maybe he had been remembering her naked, how her svelte young body moved against his own. Maybe he had butterflies in his stomach, sweat on his upper lip. And then what happened when he gave Aunty Wynn the ornament? Was either of them thinking about any of that now?

Aunty Wynn was leaning against the bonnet of her car, still

quiet. With her hands shoved deep inside her tracksuit pockets, she looked like an insolent teenager. She had flushed a deep blotchy pink. Stephen didn't say her name—he only nodded in her direction.

I felt like a kid standing between two other kids on the playground. I understood what people mean when they say *the tension was palpable.* I could sense how both of them trembled—not visibly, more like on a molecular level, like unstable matter.

Now that the three of us were there, standing in the butcher's car park, I could see that the necessary leveraging had been done. Aunty Wynn didn't care if I took over. In that moment, the handing over of the drugs that would let my mother have her peaceful death didn't mean anything to her or Stephen. The drugs were inconsequential. I was a witness to Aunty Wynn and Stephen's goodbye.

Stephen reached into his jacket pocket and withdrew the sealed glass vial of Nembutal. It was bigger than I'd pictured. He turned it over in his hand. Then he extended his hand towards me. 'I suppose you know what you're doing,' he said.

Here was the last thing we needed to do for my mother. I was impatient for the relief of having it over with, of having the vial in my possession. I held out my hand. 'We do.'

He was holding the vial just out of my reach. 'Just remember, the road to hell,' he said in a measured tone, his dimples really going for it. He was looking at Aunty Wynn.

I looked at her too.

'Don't you dare,' she said. She was doing everything in her power to sound in control.

'I'd really hate to see this go wrong,' Stephen said.

'Don't you—'

'Something with your sister, or for, I don't know, the authorities to find out.'

I looked around at the empty car park, half expecting to

see a squad of authorities creeping along the butcher's wall, or crouched and poorly hidden behind the group of decrepit shrubs on the other side of the lot, waiting for the exchange to take place, waiting to spring out and arrest us. What the hell was Stephen playing at?

'You wouldn't,' Aunty Wynn said, but she sounded unconvinced.

'Just give us the bottle and we'll be outta here,' I said.

I finally—*finally*—felt like we were doing something illegal. It had been too abstract before. Now I was genuinely worried. It turned out I was not the kind of person who got a thrill out of breaking the law, and twice in one morning. I caught the eye of Stephen's dog, who initially appeared despondent then perked up on realising she was the subject of observation. She raised her head and passionately licked the window.

'No one here is innocent,' I said, turning back to Stephen, hoping he would wake up to the fact that he was the one who had removed the drugs from his clinic. And he wasn't on his way to euthanise someone else's beloved elderly Labrador.

He shook his head profoundly, and sniggered in both a nervous and patronising way. He held the vial close to his chest. If he was gearing up to make a pathetic little moralistic speech, Aunty Wynn got in first.

'Shit,' she said. I had never heard her swear before. That word sounded frightening coming out of her mouth. 'We've been over all of this.'

'Have we?' Stephen asked. He sounded desperate now. Maybe he'd had time to picture his life without her in it, maybe he didn't like what he saw, maybe he wished he had made a different choice—a bunch of different choices.

He was turning the vial over and over in his hand now, as if it was a stress ball. I was worried he was going to drop it.

'I'm fifty-eight years old,' Aunty Wynn said. 'We've absolutely been through this.' She was clearly feeling duped. She had

thought she had signed up for one thing, and that maybe it would be sad, that maybe Stephen would be angry with her—but it was obvious she had not thought that this would happen, that he would want to continue wrestling it out with her.

'But I'm not finished,' Stephen said.

'Isn't that just life,' Aunty Wynn said.

And then, as if in agreement, Jessica contributed a short chipper bark.

That's when Stephen extended his arm once more, so he could admire the vial sitting in the palm of his large hand. A hand that had touched Aunty Wynn—all of Aunty Wynn—the blond hairs on his wrist and tops of his fingers shimmering as he closed his hand around the vial. Then abruptly he moved his hand above his head, and I sprang towards him and grabbed him by the wrist.

It was all instinct. All adrenalin. I was so fast I think I scared Stephen. I certainly scared myself. Before he let the vial go flying onto the asphalt, I extracted it. Aunty Wynn rushed at us too, placing one hand on Stephen's arm and one on mine.

What happened next was also instinct.

I was ready to walk away, but then Stephen said it: 'Bitch.'

He spoke with little conviction, and no real viciousness—it sounded almost like an apology. Another person might have felt sorry for him, because he seemed so sad and weak in that moment. I punched him.

I'd never punched anyone before. It wasn't a great punch, but it was enough to throw him off balance. After my fist connected with the bottom of his chin and I stood upright again with that vial clutched firmly in both hands, I couldn't make sense of what had happened. I couldn't believe I was the one who had hit this grown man. His sharp stubble had roughed up my knuckles—there was the proof. I took a couple of frightened steps back, maybe expecting him to come at me.

He just stood there staring at the ground. Without

acknowledging me, Aunty Wynn also took a couple of steps back. No one said anything for what felt like a very long time.

The last time I saw Karl, after we'd talked and the situation had all been laid out, when I'd turned to leave he had reached out and grabbed my arm. Hard. For what? A hug? A kiss? For one more piece? To dish out some advice? As much as I'd wanted to submit to him, to all of it, my reflex had been to laugh—a silly, weeping laugh— and then to flip him the bird. I'd felt okay leaving on that note, for all of maybe two hours. But now I wish I'd punched him. The way my left fist connected with the sharp edge of Stephen's jaw, how easy it had been not to step away, and the rush I felt as I realised how much I'd surprised Stephen with my action, if not my physical strength, made me think I could—*would*—do it again.

I held the Nembutal tight and got back inside the car, slamming the door closed behind me. The shape of the vial, its label and its brass-coloured metal seal all looked exactly as I'd thought they would.

Aunty Wynn and Stephen remained facing each other, not speaking. I was starting to shake, coming down off the adrenalin rush. I suddenly wished my mother was there. Not because I wanted to embarrass Aunty Wynn further, but because I no longer knew what might happen, and I wasn't sure I had any additional leaps of defence left in me. I felt increasingly mortified for Aunty Wynn as I watched her and Stephen out the window.

'I wanted to say,' Stephen said finally. My window was still cracked. I leaned towards the opening so I could hear him more clearly. He had retrieved that measured tone. His hands were deep inside his jacket pockets. I got the sense he wanted to touch his face, to rub where I'd hit him, but that he couldn't concede the embarrassment. 'None of this—'

The dog interrupted him. She barked a few times. We'd never owned a dog when I was growing up, as I have mild allergies,

and while I wasn't afraid of dogs I never learned how to be around them, how to read their movements. I was glad Jessica was behind a closed door.

She barked excitedly a few more times.

Stephen let her finish. 'None of this will affect Bethany's internship,' he said.

Maybe he was genuinely trying to be reassuring. But it felt more like a bitter and arrogant Post-It Note to Aunty Wynn, reminding her that despite how things had gone down they would still have to be in each other's lives. The curse of the small town.

Aunty Wynn said nothing, at least nothing that I could hear. Jessica was barking up a storm now. Some kind of madness had taken hold of her—her barks were no longer excited, they were desperate. It was as if she understood what was going on. I guess she and Aunty Wynn had spent time together. They probably had a real affection for each other. And like the goat that had bleated so rudely from the top of its hut while Aunty Wynn and I had our first standoff over my mother, Jessica couldn't remain a silent witness. Was she warning or encouraging Aunty Wynn and Stephen, though?

Either way, after having completely stolen the stage, the dog made it easier for Aunty Wynn to turn away, to leave the goodbye, that mess, alone. As she put the car in reverse, she glanced at the vial in my lap. The look on her face told me nothing.

She finally spoke when we were driving along a stretch of country road that was lined with ugly pine trees. I had my fingers out the window, which was helping to calm my stomach.

'That wasn't how I thought that would go,' she said. She was trying to sound light-hearted.

'I think I might've pictured it going worse,' I said.

'Let's split the difference then.'

'Okay. I'm going to say it went fine.'

'Me too,' Aunty Wynn said.

And that was the last either of us ever said about that morning in the car park with Stephen the vet, Jessica the Labrador and the vial of Nembutal, which was now safely wrapped up in my cardigan and stashed inside the glove compartment.

3

My mother was reclining on a beach lounger on the lawn when we arrived back at the house. She was sitting directly beneath the kitchen window, where the morning sun hit, with a grey wool blanket covering her legs. Though it wasn't very sunny out, she was wearing a large straw hat. Uncle Cliff was poking around in his gardens over the fence.

Aunty Wynn entered the house without even acknowledging my mother, and started rattling around inside the kitchen. I perched on the edge of my mother's lounger—it had cushions tied on with bows, in an awful 1970s yellow and brown floral print—using a lot of energy to keep myself upright and to stop the chair from tipping and sending her flying. On the iPad resting in her lap were photographs from the show I'd curated at Mean Space.

'How'd you get out here?' I asked. 'We've had a weird morning.'

From her expression, I could tell my mother wanted to know what had happened, but she also didn't want to hear about the adventures we had had without her. Even though everything we'd done was for her, with her on our minds, she was feeling left out. Without waiting for me to continue, she turned the iPad to face me.

I LIKE WRITING ONE. IS IT POETRY

What I'd told Aunty Wynn about the Mean Space show, my first shot at being a curator, was true: it was a painting exhibition, all geometric abstraction. There were four painters in total. Three were newish painters who had only exhibited in university-related shows or small artist-run spaces, which was

125

how I'd got to know them. There was a woman who painted thin, wobbly grids in subtle shades of grey, sand and rose, another woman whose paintings, from a distance, looked like they had been assembled out of flat fluorescent shoelaces, and a woman whose paintings were like Sonia Delaunays on a soapy spin cycle. I was a fan of their work. However, it hadn't been my decision to include the fourth painter in the show. It had been Karl's. It was this artist's painting my mother was referring to—an enormous hard-edged abstraction with lots of shattered-glass triangles in black, forest green, plum, red wine, a sun yellow straight out of the tube. These elements were already too neat, too uptight to be interesting, but to make it worse, the guy had written a short affirmation—was it poetry, or something stolen from famousquotes.com?—in the centre of the painting in neat cursive: his version of Aunty Wynn's dolphin cross-stitch hanging in the living room.

I'd got the impression that Karl owed the guy some kind of favour, and that making his intern, and the one he was screwing, find a space for him in her show of new women painters was his way of repaying it. Sure, I'd had a choice to say no, but I'd been too grateful for the opportunity to risk it. No doubt that was something Karl had banked on.

'It might be poetry, Mum,' I said now.

She was looking at another less than crisp photograph. I'd tried to capture a selection of those restrained sand- and rose-coloured grid paintings but, like a dude wearing a fedora trying to smooth-talk his way into a circle of girls at a bar, the 'poetry' painting loomed uncomfortably in the side of the frame. My mother pointed at the screen and looked at me with an expression that said, *This is impressive, right?*

'All I can tell you is that when I met the guy he was wearing a cricket sweater—one of those white woollen V-necks. And he had one of these moustaches.'

She searched my face as I illustrated the kind of moustache I meant. She didn't grasp my point. I didn't want to get into what that guy's painting was doing in my show—that would have involved sidling up to a confession about Karl—but I couldn't lie about his work being any good. My mother continued to swipe through more installation shots, photos of individual paintings, a couple of extreme close-ups—they really weren't great images, just snaps I'd taken with my phone. Karl had organised for a professional to document the show, but I hadn't seen those photographs yet.

'What do you think about the other three painters?' I asked.

She had obviously anticipated this question, or something like it. She brought up another note.

FLUORO ONES ARE A BIT OUT THERE. LIGHT ONES ARE LIKE WONKY MATHS PAPER

'Yeah, the fluoro ones are cool,' I said.

I took her comment as positive: those fluoros *were* garish, but excitingly so. They bumped up against the paintings by the two other women in a way that was pleasantly annoying. I'd started pulling out clumps of grass from the lawn around my feet and irritably throwing them away. I'd created intentional discord. It was entirely different from what Karl had done to my show.

'Hold on a second,' I said.

The lawn was cold and damp with dew, and there were pieces of grass stuck to my hands. I wiped them across the knees of my jeans before I stole back my mother's iPad, swiping till I found the photo I was thinking of.

It was a detail shot of one of the fluoro shoelace paintings. The photo revealed some depths that weren't evident from across the room. You could see the edge of each brushstroke, thick like frosting. And there were quieter layers behind those loud top strokes. The colours that poked out from below were

much more contained, dignified—soft blues and purples, a calm cool green. My mother inspected it sincerely. She seemed to nod.

'Bet you didn't expect that,' I said.

She didn't reply, though she didn't swipe away from the photo either.

'The woman who painted them got so drunk at the opening she broke her ankle.'

My mother was obviously pleased by this detail.

As I mentioned, the opening wasn't exactly a hit. People stayed long enough to drink the free alcohol, the fluoro shoelace painter had actually fallen from her chair while dancing at an unrelated party after the opening, and really only a handful of colleagues from the Art History Department had made the effort to share any positive comments about the show. However, despite the painting that Karl had muscled in, I felt good about what I'd put together.

My mother had something else to add.

WHAT ABOUT SOME BIG COLOURFUL SCULPTURES ON FLOOR

I should have been grateful that she was at least engaging with what I'd done. I guess there are a lot of parents who aren't interested enough in their child's work to even want to advise them on how to do it better. What got under my skin was the fact that she was using a pre-typed statement instead of responding to what I'd shared with her in real time.

'But I didn't want to fill the floor,' I said.

In truth, sculpture scared me. The canvas made me feel confident that there was a world order by which I could organise what I saw. Sculptural paintings were one thing, but the idea that sculptural sculpture could be anything—anything!—made me feel physically ill. I sure as hell wouldn't know how to know whether it was any good. Or where on the floor it should go.

Or if it should even go on the floor. Were plinths still passé?

This cowardice might also help explain why I had chosen Rita Angus as the central subject of my master's thesis. My mother had enquired about how this was progressing the night I arrived. I was on track with my word count, so I told her it was going well. The problem was I'd failed to take any worthwhile risks. Now that I had only a semester to go, and maybe because of everything that had happened recently, I could finally admit it to myself. I'd wanted to write about someone else—a painter who was still alive, and whom I thought of as New Zealand's Helen Frankenthaler, although their working styles were fundamentally different—but, at the last minute, I'd changed my proposal to focus on a group of Angus's claustrophobic Wellington paintings. I'd felt lukewarm about these pieces at the beginning, and now I loathed them. My thesis was adequately researched and thoughtfully written, but it might have been fresher if I'd had the guts to articulate some of my disdain.

Now I was crashing down off my little high, my little feeling good about myself. I hated how easily my mother could take the wind out of me like that.

Everything she had said to me at the beginning of her diagnosis about how life needed to go on as usual, how nothing about our relationship should change—I'd not expected that to remain true. Maybe for other people facing down a terminal illness it isn't true, or can't stay true, but for the most part my mother had kept her word. Our relationship hadn't fundamentally changed. This was something I would come to admire, though not in that moment. Why couldn't she have melted into a slightly cuddlier, more patient, more generous mother? Even if only because this was the second-to-last day of her life?

Then again, who was I to expect those things?

I leaned over and placed the vial of Nembutal in her lap.

'We got the stuff anyway.' I was surprised by how cross I sounded.

Before I could register her response, a small moth flew out from between the folds of the wool blanket that was covering her legs and headed directly for her face. She pulled away from it with such force that her iPad went flying onto the grass near my feet.

'It's only a house moth,' I said, waving the tiny creature off. I retrieved the iPad, which was a little wet but fine.

She screwed up her face, did her best to flap her arms at the tiny insect that had already flown away. She was afraid of moths. Butterflies too. Whenever one got trapped inside our house, I was the one who had to deal to it. Usually I would capture the creature with a jar and a piece of card, then release it outside. If it was late or the moth was playing hard to get, I would have to resort to a blow with a tea towel. She only ever asked me to be careful when it was a monarch butterfly.

'I know they're meant to be special, sacred,' she said to me once, 'but I think they're hideous.'

'Worse than cockroaches?' I said.

'It's the way they come right at you,' she said, ignoring my comparison. She illustrated with her hands a butterfly's jerky attack. 'The unsure, aggressive movements.'

'So if they flew with more conviction?'

She started batting at the air between us, fighting off an imaginary butterfly. 'And then the tongues!' she said, cringing.

I have no idea how she dealt with moths after I moved out. I can imagine her fortifying herself with a gin and tonic, selecting the largest, fluffiest towel from the cupboard, and then just charging at it, crushing the poor confused thing to dust.

'If you held that blanket up to the light,' I said now, as I was

drying off the iPad on my T-shirt, 'it would probably look like the side of a box grater.'

She shuddered. She was still trying to gauge where the moth was.

'It's gone,' I said.

'You're fine.'

She tried to lift the blanket away from her legs. 'Do you want me to shake it out?'

She wanted to say yes—I could sense the tension in her body— but she shook her head, as if suddenly feeling silly.

'Here,' I said, placing the iPad back in her lap.

Only then did she acknowledge the vial of Nembutal, which thankfully hadn't been bothered by her fussing. For a moment I couldn't decipher the look on her face. Was it lingering alarm from her brief encounter with the moth, or her realising what that vial meant? She stared at it, then she covered it with her hand, and I didn't see her look at it again.

Here was a different kind of fear entirely.

I couldn't remember the last time we had sat outside on a lawn together. It must have been years, some summer afternoon long ago in our garden in Wellington, the wind whipping up. Maybe we'd lasted five minutes before it got too cold, our hair blowing around our faces and into our cups of tea. It wasn't warm out there on Aunty Wynn's lawn either, but the sun was bright and there was no wind. Besides a couple of birds chirruping, the world felt calm. God, how that calm rocked me.

That calm, and my mother's slow taps on her iPad.

I turned so I could see Uncle Cliff bent over his tractor-tyre gardens. I still wanted to ask him for a ride on his horse. I had a romantic vision of how that animal would feel beneath me, with my hair swept back from my face and all my worries flying off me. I tried not to think of the terrible horse stories I'd heard

about people being thrown, trampled, their skulls imprinted with a deep crescent.

Seeing Uncle Cliff's back to me reminded me of what he had said about the painting I'd stolen from Craig. Though that problem felt very remote right then. Having finally handed over the drugs to my mother, I was more concerned about how we would fill the time between that afternoon and the following evening. I'd walked to the edge of the ravine now. Would the vertigo get to me?

My mother finally looked up. She looked tired. She turned the iPad screen to face me, but before I could read anything she changed her mind, pulled it back. Then she continued typing. A few more minutes passed. I didn't want to be impatient, but she seemed to have floated off into her own world. She wasn't writing for conversation; she was writing for herself.

'Is there something you want me to read?' I asked.

Without looking up, she gave me a thumbs down. I can't imagine what was going through her mind now that she had what she wanted, now that at any point she could slip away. I hoped she wouldn't slip away without me—tonight, for example, while I slept— but she could. She could do what she liked now. Since I'd ticked off everything on her innocuous list—the flowers, the music, the relocating of the dolphins— and now that all the preparations had been made, I supposed I was meant to return to the sidelines to wait it all out. I remained uncertain about what to expect from tomorrow, but I'd gotten used to the idea that I had a part to play, that I was an important cog in this clumsy death machine.

I'd gotten comfortable with the idea that my mother's death belonged to me too. But it was clear that that wasn't the case. And I had no right.

I returned to the kitchen where Aunty Wynn was eating from a

plate set with four kinds of crackers and a tower of cheese slices. The radio was off. The trampoline over the fence was empty. The Queen's Birthday chicken was defrosting in a plastic bowl in the sink. I helped myself to some of Aunty Wynn's cheese and crackers. We both stared out the window in silence.

I couldn't see my mother's face, only her sun hat, shoulders, the top part of her iPad screen, and the blanket covering her legs. I wondered what she was typing and for whom. I was feeling bitter at the thought that it might not be for me, when I saw her hand awkwardly adjust her hat. And as with so many other times recently, she felt very far away from me, adrift on her own lake of pain and frustration. The way her hand inexpertly pulled at that brim, making it better or maybe making it worse, was like a miserable tipping of a hat to the end. And still she was tugging at it, the movement as if a junior puppeteer was operating her limb with strings and pulleys.

I looked away. 'You want a cup of tea?' I asked Aunty Wynn.

She had taken another slice of cheese, another cracker, a round one this time, and put both in her mouth. She was chewing slowly. It was an exaggerated display. God, she took a long time to munch up that cracker and cheese slice, much longer than necessary, as if she had lost her teeth and was using only her gums.

When she eventually swallowed, she said—her voice like that of someone giving testimony in court for a grisly crime, both cold and shaking with emotion—'He called me a bitch.'

I reached for another cracker. At the same time Aunty Wynn snatched away the plate. Then she turned and shuffled from the kitchen in something close to a death shuffle. It was as if over the course of that morning she had aged twenty years.

It was then that I had the idea to show my mother the painting I'd stolen. I needed something to do, but I also realised that I'd actually enjoyed having her tell me how I could improve on something that I'd done once and that she had never done. The

frustration I'd felt was so ingrained in our relationship, and it was a feeling entirely free of any of the pity or sadness or frightening anger that had tinged much in our lives since last February. Sitting on that lounger I'd simply been a woman felled by her mother. No one told me how much I would miss being that kind of annoyed, that kind of hurt. And it was preferable to standing alone in the kitchen with nothing to do, no one to talk to. So I left the kettle and returned to Bethany's bedroom. Though when I opened the cupboard where I'd hidden the painting that morning, the painting wasn't there.

Aunty Wynn had prepared a boiled chicken for Queen's Birthday lunch for as long as I could remember. My mother provided the following indictment every year: 'That my sister would boil a chicken instead of roasting it shows how fundamentally screwed up her priorities are.' For a long time the boiled chicken had been a line in the sand between Aunty Wynn and my mother and me: the line we would never cross, and the line Aunty Wynn could never cross because she didn't know it existed.

I watched this year's chicken through the glass lid of the pot as it boiled. It was my job to boil the eggs—a simple task that was either a gift or punishment, I wasn't sure which. Aunty Wynn was scrubbing potatoes beside me, and Bethany was julienning carrots for a salad. My mother was awkwardly slumped in one of the mustard-coloured kitchen chairs, her legs stretched out on another, her walker within reach. The four Moore women preparing food together—that was something that had never previously happened and which I would not have predicted.

Bethany was making hard work of the carrots. She didn't appear at all hungover, despite the large amounts of cheap booze I'd watched her drink the night before. Her work was precise—the carrot sticks looked like they had come through

a machine—but in the twenty minutes we'd been together, she had only cut up one carrot. Aunty Wynn was in a strange mood, alternately encouraging everyone in her usual upbeat style and plummeting into sullen silences. My mother just sat and watched, looking amused. When I asked if I could help her move to a more comfortable chair, she insisted, through a series of gestures, that she was fine and I was fussing.

I watched the six eggs bounce around the pan of boiling water. Though they gave me something simple to focus on, I was getting worried about the whereabouts of the painting, waiting for the other shoe to drop. I'd reasoned some stupid explanations, wondering whether I'd stolen the painting at all, or if I'd dreamt the whole thing. I also wondered whether Craig might have broken into the house that morning and stolen it back. Or had Bethany seen it while rummaging through her cupboard and done something drastic with it? I didn't know who to talk to, who to rope into this drama I'd created for myself. Uncle Cliff was the only person who could vouch for what I'd done, but when I'd tried to find him he was no longer in his garden or answering the door of his sleep-out.

'It was so funny,' Bethany said now. She was talking about how she and Brent had tried to spend the night in the teepee. They had dragged the lawn chairs inside with their sleeping bags, but it had still gotten too cold, and then Brent had had to go home anyway.

'What about the fire?' I asked, remembering how it had been smoking when I left.

'Oh yeah, it died eventually,' Bethany said. She pinched one perfect carrot matchstick between two fingers. She was grinning, her braces front and centre. 'Imagine if we'd carbon-dioxided ourselves to death.'

'What's that?' Aunty Wynn said. 'What're you talking about?'

'Nothing,' Bethany said. She eased her way through one more meticulous carrot stick.

'Isn't the carrot usually grated?' I asked, not concealing my frustration.

Bethany shrugged. She had glimpsed enough of my troubles to know I wasn't as intimidating as she might have thought two days ago. She started to move even slower with her knife.

'She's doing a fine job,' Aunty Wynn said.

'If you say so,' I said.

'If I'm going to make it as a surgical vet, I need to have a steady hand,' Bethany said.

'That's very true,' Aunty Wynn said, though I thought I heard her voice wobble.

'Steady does it,' Bethany said to herself as she started working on another matchstick. 'Have you seen the size of a pygmy marmoset?' she asked, in all seriousness.

'I imagine they're very small?' Aunty Wynn said, talking vacantly now, no longer 100% in the room with us.

'Smaller than Ringo.' Bethany reached across and picked up one of the wet potatoes Aunty Wynn had been scrubbing. 'Smaller than this,' she said, thrusting the potato in my direction. 'Imagine performing surgery on this. If you can.'

It was my turn to shrug now. Bethany blew a lanky piece of hair out of her eyes and my mother snorted. I turned my back on the boiling eggs so I could face her—she was snorting with glee.

'I'm glad you're having fun,' I said.

My mother made her best attempt at a smirk then. Though I couldn't say why, it felt like she was punishing me. Our usual approach to Queen's Birthday lunch was that she and I took sides against the others. She was enjoying mucking up those lines—lines that had been entirely mucked up since Saturday, but I still felt hurt.

'Just chill, Erin,' Bethany said. Then she burst out laughing. It was horrendous—a teenage bully's laugh.

I felt idiotic. I couldn't think of anything clever to say. I

turned my attention back to the eggs, and then to the sound of a car coming up the driveway. It wasn't Uncle Cliff's truck. Two car doors opened and closed, and there was the shape of that navy hat with its wide lid, black brim and chequerboard trim with the coat of arms in the middle, as it cruised past the kitchen window. And then another hat, and two faces turned up to the window so I could just make out two pairs of large reflective sunglasses, the kind cyclists and marathon runners wear.

Even before the knock, before Bethany answered the door, I knew what was about to happen. As I waited, the stupidity of what I'd done rose to the surface. I turned back to the oven, one eye on the eggs, one eye on the boiling chicken, its loosening flesh, and I knew I was about to find out the extent of the trouble I'd made for myself and everyone else in that house.

The two police officers, a man and a woman, were tall, distinctly bottom heavy, the pleats in their navy-blue slacks straining. They were standing a few steps inside the kitchen. Peering out from behind them, Bethany looked extremely guilty. My mother couldn't clearly see what was going on, but I could see the expression on her face: she knew the police had arrived.

Aunty Wynn was on high alert. 'Excuse the mess,' she said. Without prompting she reached for the electric kettle and started filling it from the tap. 'It's our annual family get-together. Please help yourselves to a seat. How d'you take your tea?' She spoke too quickly and confidently, as if she had rehearsed this scene in front of a mirror. It gave her the overly casual appearance of the culpable.

The officers hadn't yet told us what they wanted. Both removed their hats and sunglasses before the woman spoke.

'No tea for us thanks,' she said, without smiling.

'Is th—' the man started.

The room waited while he focused on a spot above my head, his mouth open, his tongue at attention, as if he was trying to remember his lines. He looked annoyed. The kitchen heater made its presence known with a loud couple of ticks.

'—this th—the Moore residence?'

'That's correct,' Aunty Wynn said, unflinching.

Still standing behind the officers, Bethany looked as if she was making a list in her head of all the small crimes she had committed. Maybe also picturing a kid with a stutter whom she had once bullied. She looked sweaty.

None of them—my mother, Aunty Wynn, Bethany—knew

about the painting. If they had, they might have been able to look less guilty. Though there were also the other crimes: the one involving the extortion of the Nembutal, and the yet-to-be-committed one involving my mother's use of it. Each was worth up to fourteen years for Aunty Wynn and me. I could get another seven for stealing the painting. Though I wasn't aware of the extent of those numbers at the time, and even when confronted with the very real prospect of doing some kind of *time*, it was still, surprisingly, outside the frame of what I could imagine for myself. I'd only drawn a large, loose circle around the presumption that I could *get in trouble*. So, on par with a child who has spilled cranberry juice on the carpet.

'We understand an Erin Moore is staying here at present?' the woman said.

I put up my hand. 'Present.'

It probably seemed like I was being impertinent, but I was thrown on hearing my name spoken in full by a cop. I wanted to cooperate.

'There's been an incident on—' The officer took a small notepad from her slacks pocket. 'Freshfields Meadow,' she said, looking up. 'We'd like to talk to you about it.'

'Down at th—the station,' her colleague said.

'Absolutely,' I said, too jolly.

I looked at my mother then. It was clear that despite what the officer had explained, she still thought the police arriving at the house to speak to me had everything to do with what I'd done for her. She looked panicked, and seeing her panicked made me feel panicked.

'The eggs!' I said. They suddenly seemed important. There were a couple more minutes on the timer, and then there was the next stage of the process, which Aunty Wynn had insisted on withholding. What were we making? Egg salad, devilled eggs, just good old boiled eggs? I didn't know. Eggs had never featured at Queen's Birthday lunch before.

Aunty Wynn was arranging cups beside the kettle, as well as a selection of teas, milk and sugar. She was completely absorbed by the task.

'I'll do the eggs,' Bethany said, so quietly that the woman started, obviously having forgotten about the girl who had answered the door.

'Okay. Thanks. I just gotta put my shoes on,' I said, and the woman watched as I went to retrieve my sneakers from the shoe pile beside the kitchen door.

None of us had asked what had happened on Freshfields Meadow, which must have seemed strange, troubling. I was more concerned about how the other officer was rubbernecking around the kitchen, and now a foot into the dining room, now the hallway. If he entered my mother's bedroom he would see the vial of Nembutal, sitting plain as day on the bedside table.

My shoes weren't in the pile. I'd either kicked them off in my mother's room or Bethany's room. If I went looking for them the officer might follow, and maybe he would see the glass vial on my mother's bedside table and think it looked suspicious. Maybe he wouldn't, but it was a gamble I couldn't take. I picked up the pair of shoes closest to me: Aunty Wynn's orange Nikes. They were much too big, and as I crouched in the middle of the kitchen to tie the laces as tight as I could—worrying about what would happen if I had to run somewhere and whether I would come flying out of these boats—I could hear the eggs bouncing around their stainless-steel pan.

That sound still gives me the cold sweats.

When I stood back up, Bethany was staring at my feet. I caught her eye, bit down hard on my bottom lip, and looked away. My heart was racing. Aunty Wynn was leaning against the kitchen counter wearing an insane cheerful expression. She moved the line of teacups into a more orderly line. The officer who had been nosing around was back and standing close by.

My mother. My mother looked stricken.

'Okay, that's me,' I said, looking both officers square in the eye.

The man said, haltingly, that someone should follow us to the station.

'So you can get home,' the woman said.

The suggestion that I would eventually be coming home only made the prospect of not coming home seem all the more likely.

'Is she arrested?' Bethany asked, sounding how I felt.

'She is not,' the woman said. 'We just want a talk at this stage.'

Bethany nodded solemnly. 'About what exactly?'

The officer didn't get a chance to respond because everyone in the room turned to look at my mother, who was trying to stand up. She had thrown one arm towards her walker and was trying to twist around in her chair and speak.

I couldn't decipher what was coming out of her mouth. She sounded much worse than the last time I'd heard her speak. It was awful to hear.

The man screwed up his face.

'Are you okay, ma'am?' the woman asked.

My mother rolled her eyes, spoke again.

It was worse the second time because she was getting frustrated now too. Was she trying to confess? Was she trying to unload some urgent motherly advice? Was she trying to tell me, for the first time in my adult life, that she loved me?

'I can't tell what you're saying,' I said quietly.

'Is she okay?' the woman asked the room.

'She's okay,' I said. But my mind was buckling. What if I really didn't make it back for tomorrow? Or, worse, what if the arrival of the police killed my mother's nerve and she couldn't follow through? My mother's wish for a peaceful death on Tuesday evening in the house where she had grown up was like a poorly constructed fire that had been lit in my chest on Saturday afternoon when I stood beneath that pōhutukawa with Aunty

Wynn. Since then, though the fire hadn't always been strong, though it had sometimes been pathetic, barely a whimper of a fire, it had remained burning and I'd gotten used to it. And now I felt as if it had been doused with kerosene so it roared with a ferocity that made me feel wild and protective, not of my mother, exactly, but of what she wanted, that one thing she had asked of us, the one thing I could protect.

'She's okay,' I said again, my throat thick, far from the authoritative tone I was shooting for. 'She has MND.'

'Have you t—taken something you shouldn't have?' the man asked without acknowledging my comment. He bent towards my mother in a patronising way, as if speaking to an infant, or, worse, as Stephen the vet might have spoken to Jessica the Labrador on catching her snacking on the contents of a trash can.

That flipped Aunty Wynn out of her cordiality. 'She's not intoxicated,' she snapped. 'She's got a neurodegenerative disease.' And she swooped across the kitchen, pushed my mother back into her chair and gave her shoulders a good squeeze.

Aunty Wynn the matriarch, Aunty Wynn the mama bear, the top hen, the queen sow, the prize bitch, the bitchin'est mare, the most killer lioness, had returned. And in wild defence mode. Then she grabbed me by the shoulders and, while steering me out of the house, informed the officers that she would follow right behind. It wasn't till I saw her from the back of the police car that I noticed she was getting into her car barefoot.

The police interview room was less like the dim, cinder-block interrogation rooms you see on TV and more like one of the bright music practice rooms at my old high school. There was a table with a hard chair either side, as you might expect, but all four walls were covered with cheap wavy grey foam. There

was also an upright piano against the back wall.

Only the woman joined me. She brought with her a yellow notepad and pen, a plastic cup of water (for herself; I'd not been offered one) and a compact recording device. After turning on the recorder and stating her name, my name, the date and time, she started with broad strokes: what my day job was, my reason for visiting Aunty Wynn, how long I planned on staying, etcetera. She made notes as I answered. They were easy questions. I believed I would do anything to protect my mother's wish, to not mess this up for her. Though I wasn't 100% sure what that looked like.

Eventually the officer moved on to Craig.

'How well do you know Mr Green?' she asked.

'Not well,' I said.

'Though you've been to his house?'

'Yes, he lives across the paddock from my family,' I said, my voice catching as I recalled the exact place I'd met him: on top of his fence, mid-trespass. 'We met by chance. Yesterday for the first time.'

She nodded. 'Do you know why we want to speak to you?'

I said I didn't. My loose plan, which I'd formed on the journey to the police station, was this: deny everything. I wouldn't admit to anything more than having gone to Craig's house, having a drink with him, crashing out on the couch due to exhaustion (*My mother is very ill, it's very stressful*). And it wouldn't be lying to say I didn't know where the painting was—I could testify to that in court.

'Mr Green believes you've stolen something from him.'

I raised my eyebrows theatrically, suggesting she should continue because I couldn't for the life of me imagine what that thing might be. My guts rolled like eels in a tank.

'A painting,' she added. 'Apparently it's worth a lot to him. Do you know anything about that?'

'A painting?' I asked, incredulous. 'Of what?'

The officer flicked back through her notes and read the following: 'An approximately 50 centimetres by 40 centimetres painting on canvas with no discernible subject, with brown being the dominant colour, with pink, yellow and grey being the secondary colours. No frame. Signature on the back: C. Green, 1974.' She looked up. 'Do you remember seeing a painting fitting that description when you visited Mr Green?'

I told her I didn't. I'd never thought of myself as a liar—I'd been nervous about how well I could pull off the lie I'd thought out. I certainly hadn't planned on denying the existence of the painting, so I was alarmed by how quickly the lie started to take on a life of its own.

'You sure about that?' the officer asked. She was trying to figure out if I was stupid enough to think I could get away with lying to the police.

'I'm sure,' I said. No turning back now. 'And I only met Mr Green yesterday, but I didn't get the impression he was the kind of person who cared about art.'

It occurred to me that Mr Green was one of the characters in the murder mystery game *Cluedo* that I'd played as a kid. Was that why the more the officer referred to Craig as Mr Green, and now that I'd said it out loud, too, the easier it was for me to lie, to feign ignorance? The whole interaction felt increasingly unreal, deceivingly low stakes. I was starting to feel on top.

'I'll be back,' the officer said finally, abruptly tapping her notepad on the desk. She took the recorder and untouched cup of water with her too.

It was a small police station—only a few rooms off a narrow hallway. With its low ceiling, fluorescent lights and ugly grey carpet the room could have been a very depressing accountant's office, excluding the foam insulation. There was no one-way window nestled in that wavy grey wall, which might have been what had inspired someone to try to graffiti it with a thick black marker. That same person had also tried to graffiti the piano,

though it looked like they had been stopped mid-tag, as next to the incomplete word there was a badly stylised illustration of the half-rampant lion you usually see on the front of a Holden. I tried to imagine the kind of person who would think it wise to tag a brand of truck inside a police station. A very young person? A very stupid person? What might they have been questioned about? Was it worse than what I'd done? Were they in prison now? Anyway, I was no better.

The other officer entered the room. He had his own yellow notepad and pen and cup of water. He returned the recorder to the desk, switched it on.

'T—tell me about this painting,' he said.

'I don't know anything about it,' I said. 'Just what your colleague said.'

'Yet you're studying art history? You probably know something about th—'

There was a long, painful silence, while the officer tried to get the rest of his question out. During that silence he was no longer able to maintain eye contact with me. He focused on the wall over my shoulder.

'—this artist?'

'No, I don't,' I said.

Though it was true I knew nothing about the artist, from the beginning it was easier for me to lie to this officer than to the other one. Maybe because I'd had some practice. However, the further we got into the interview the worse the officer's stutter got. It started to throw me.

The officer again fixed his gaze on a spot on the far wall as he asked me why I thought Craig had accused me of stealing his painting. He looked at me when he was done.

'I couldn't say,' I said.

'How d'you—' Looking enraged, and after a short silence, he seemed to change tack. 'And in th—the morning after you left Mr Green's?'

I was starting to feel all kinds of bad about what I'd taken for granted my whole life. My whole life, that is, until the moment when my mother had started to lose her ability to speak—something that this man had clearly never been in the position to take for granted. I felt spoilt. We'd all been spoilt.

The officer seemed to sense how uncomfortable his stutter was making me. When he made eye contact with me now, I thought I saw a glint.

'Apologies,' he said, waving his hand in front of his mouth.

Was I on the receiving end of some kind of very nuanced good cop/bad cop routine?

'No, no worries,' I said. 'This morning after I left Mr Green's?'

Though it had been in my original plan, I didn't remember telling either officer that I'd spent the night at Craig's house. I'd also failed to come up with a good lie for what I was doing when Aunty Wynn and I were completing our transaction with Stephen the vet. I'd neglected to even think about it. Why hadn't Aunty Wynn and I discussed a cover story?

We'd been too sure of ourselves, that's why. Amateur hour.

The officer nodded. 'Between seven and ten.'

'I was at home,' I said. 'At my aunty's house I mean.'

'You sure?' the officer asked.

'Yes,' I said, realising—with a violent stirring of that tank of eels— that I'd now effortlessly rolled Aunty Wynn and my mother up in my lie. There was no way for Aunty Wynn to know what to say if they questioned her on my whereabouts. She was just as likely to spin a tale placing both of us in the butcher's car park that morning.

'So what d—'

Each time the next syllable failed to come out or there was a long gap between one sound and the next, the officer's mouth open, his neck rigid, both of us avoiding eye contact as we waited for him to finish, a deepening canyon opened up between us: one I felt I could very easily throw myself into.

The officer wanted to know what I was doing at Aunty Wynn's house during that time.

'I had breakfast and hung out with my mum,' I said. 'Then I was feeling tired so I had a nap. You arrived while we were cooking lunch.'

When I wasn't looking the officer in the eye I'd been staring at my hands and picking at the dirt from beneath my fingernails. Now I caught sight of Aunty Wynn's bright orange shoes, crossed under the table. Those were not my feet on the end of my legs. This was not a conversation I'd ever imagined having. Was stealing that painting really what I would go down for? Was this to be my legacy? I didn't feel like myself. And then picture a puddle on a footpath slick with oil and rimmed with trash, now illuminated by a bold ray of sunshine so the dog turd dropped centre emerges clear as day. That was how I felt on recalling what I'd said to Craig the night before, about my mother wanting to die on Tuesday. I'd stolen his painting, yes, but had I also invited the police to sniff around about my mother? Would Craig have remembered anything, and managed to join any dots? Would Stephen the vet really have gone to the authorities? Had I helped make the thing that I'd most worried about come true?

'He leaves his kitchen door open for his cat,' I said.

'Mr Green?' the officer asked, perfectly clearly.

'Yes,' I said. 'So the cat can come in and out. If someone was going to take something from him, it wouldn't be hard—it could've happened any time.'

There was no denying that remembering that detail at that point in the interview, and the way I blurted it out, rather than being an excellent piece of defence, made me sound like I had something to hide.

Now it was this officer's turn to get up and leave. He lumbered out with no urgency at all, forgetting to close the door behind him. Rather than being trapped in the soundproof room with

only my own lies, I heard the tense sounds of a man being questioned nearby. Someone else had failed to close a door. From what I could gather, the man had been caught snooping around outside some woman's bedroom window, though he was denying these accusations—his defence was something to do with his cat.

'He's been shitting all over our lawn,' he said. 'Every few days my wife makes me go out and pick it all up. We saw him shitting on the neighbour's lawn too.'

'So you went over to pick it up?'

'As much as I could without trespassing. I was kneeling on our shared pathway.'

He sounded on the verge of tears—both out of fear and what was clearly a blinding rage towards the cat.

'What's the cat's name?' the officer asked. He sounded sceptical.

'Lentil.'

'And what kind of cat is Lentil?'

'A regular cat, what do you call them? A tabby? With white socks.'

'So when your neighbour woke and saw you crouched outside her bedroom window with your raincoat on, the hood up, staring in, you were in fact just scouting her lawn for accessible, ah, cat shit?'

'Yes.'

'In the rain?'

'Yes. Look—a large tomcat has been coming onto our property,' the man said. 'I think it's been scaring our cat. I think he's been trying to mark his territory or something.'

'Do cats do that?' the officer asked.

The interrogation was excruciating to listen to. The officer's tone gave nothing away. Though I couldn't see the man being questioned, he didn't sound very old; a young man at the start of his life, marriage, with a bunch of plans and dreams, who was

now being questioned about something that could, I imagined, get his name on a sex-offender registry. I was convinced by his story for no reason other than it seemed much too weird a lie to be a lie. And that worried me. Maybe because I'd just spun a bunch of dull lies to my officers, it didn't seem fair that both of us should walk out of this police station.

The woman officer returned to my room before I got to hear what happened next. She closed the door behind her, placed her notepad and pen, tape recorder and cup of water on the table, leaned back in her chair and looked at me as if we'd never met.

'Can you tell me again what you did this morning after you left Mr Green's house?' she asked.

I repeated my story. This time the officer didn't take any notes—she just listened. And this time, rather than feeling more comfortable with my story, really settling into it and selling the fact that I'd stayed in, hung out with my mother, had a nap, and, if she asked about the painting again, preparing myself to convincingly lie about how I didn't know anything about it, I felt completely unpersuasive. I felt wooden.

When I was done the officer planted her elbows on the table, hands out like someone threatening an arm wrestle. It was as if she could smell how close I was to crumbling.

'Tell me,' she said, 'what made you remember that detail about Mr Green leaving his kitchen door open?'

If the other officer hadn't opened the door just then and gestured to his colleague to join him in the hallway, I don't know what I might have said. I'd felt the truth rising up the back of my throat.

So there I was, alone again. I felt sick. And claustrophobic. The wavy grey walls weren't helping. And what was a piano doing in a police interview room anyway? I tried to make out the conversation between the two officers, to get a sense of what might be coming next, but I couldn't decipher anything they

were saying. What I could hear was what was happening with the cat-shit guy. His officer had the man's wife on the phone now—this was evident by the way he ended every question with 'ma'am', the same questions he had asked the man earlier. And maybe because the officer was getting the same answers from her as her husband, answers he didn't like— who would like their noble career being reduced to chasing up about a cat with a willy-nilly sphincter?—he was growing frustrated and loud.

'So what you're saying, ma'am, is that you sent your husband out into the rain to pick up after your cat? … And please tell me, ma'am, where were you while this was happening? … I wouldn't say it was normal behaviour, ma'am.'

Now the woman officer returned. She looked exasperated. She didn't close the door or sit down. She reminded me a lot of Aunty Wynn, the way she stood with both hands on her hips: the woman of the station.

'You can go,' she said. 'Your aunty's waiting in reception.'

What had happened? Where was the painting, or where did the police think it was? What about all those questions about how I'd spent my morning? Did they know something about what Aunty Wynn and I had been up to? Were they letting me go so they could catch us in a trap later?

As I followed the officer from the room, my mind spinning, and maybe because I also felt wildly relieved, I asked her, 'What's the deal with the piano?'

She waved her hand disinterestedly around the room. 'It's soundproof,' she said. Out in the hallway she added, 'We'll be in touch if we have any other questions.'

From around the middle of puberty, being athletic started to have less social value and my stocks began a steady downwards slide. Being a pretty good swimmer—I was starting to win

medals in national competitions—didn't mean much to the guys at the pool, or the guys I crushed on outside of the pool complex. I didn't swim because I wanted a boyfriend, but I was surprised to realise that looking good in the water didn't mean I was any more attractive on land.

I don't know where my desire to become an artist came from, but when I landed on it—*Artist*—I guess I thought it might make me special. No one else at the pool did art or even cared about it. I started keeping a 'diary' where I sketched pictures of the only things I could think of: glossy fruit, candles, moist eyes emanating whorls and squiggles. When I started taking art courses at high school—painting, print-making—my subject matter shifted to trees, fences, shrubs in front of fences, domestic still lifes hovering in front of landscapes of trees and shrubs and, sometimes, the sea. I was scared of abstraction then. Yet I assumed I was talented enough to get into the art school of my choice. I wasn't. And it said something about my confidence (or delusion) that I was astounded when I didn't get a single interview, not even for my second- and third-choice schools. And I still didn't have a boyfriend.

I think I believed that my predisposition for hard work, for a solo, repetitive life—everything that had made me a pretty good swimmer—should have made me a good artist. I'd swum because I loved to swim. I loved the repetition of it. I loved the competition. I loved winning. And the pain, the pain became something to love, too. My water bottle carried the slogan *No Pain No Gain*, pink text on turquoise. But as my coach flatly pointed out, I didn't have the X-factor, the buckets of raw talent that would transform my hard work—that pain, those national-level medals—into something extraordinary, singular.

My mother was the one to suggest I pursue art history. I liked researching and writing about art, and now curating shows. And while none of it was the same as being the artist, the one in the arena, for the most part I'd made peace with my

failure, as well as the thought that I might only ever be so-so at this too.

In some ways, I think that my lack of talent, the fact that I'd tried and failed at being an artist, might have made me love art more. Similarly, I still think about a race I saw during the last Olympics. It was the women's 400 IM final, and a swimmer from Hungary was out front. By her second length of backstroke I had goosebumps. When she touched the wall at the end of the freestyle a lump had formed in my throat and I had tears in my eyes. She had demolished the world record, which was impressive, but it was how she had done it that got me—she had sprinted the entire race. It was an astonishing exhibition of power, stamina, and elegance. I'm not certain that trying and failing to make art, in the piddly way I'd tried and failed, made me any better at being able to recognise a good painting, let alone an extraordinary one, though was that part of why I'd unhooked that painting in Craig's living room? Because I wanted to prove that I knew what I was talking about, that my failure hadn't been for nothing, that I had something to give?

During the police interview it had occurred to me that stealing the painting could be the thing I would go down for, and I'll admit that the thought of this—the idea of me that people might have, as a kind of Robin Hood of paintings—had pleased me some. What had I really hoped to gain, though? Surely I knew that everything I'd just gone through—that horrible interview experience—would be the best-case scenario? Yes, and on one hand I think I simply made a stupid, thoughtless mistake. On the other hand, I think I had also needed to do something brazen, something insane that would make what was happening with my mother feel a little less insane. And maybe I believed that if I could get away with that one crime, then we might get away with the others—and not only that, but we might have something of worth to look back on too.

So if we did get away with it all, what picture did I hope to see?

Of my mother on her deathbed, of my mother killing herself while Aunty Wynn and I watched? What final interpretation, what rendering of these events could I imagine hanging on my wall and looking at every single day for the rest of my life?

5

Aunty Wynn handed me a large plastic-wrapped biscuit as we pulled out of the police station parking lot. The biscuit was loaded with chocolate chips and dried apricot. Although I was ravenous, I made hard work of picking out the apricot cubes and collecting them in a lump in the palm of my hand. Aunty Wynn didn't say a word. When I eventually snuck a sideways glance in her direction, expecting to see the muscles in her jaw kneading against her cheeks while she figured out what she wanted to say, I was disappointed to see that she looked completely calm.

'Thanks for that,' I said, concealing the sweaty wad of apricot in the wrapper. 'I was starving.'

Still nothing.

Further down the road we passed the paddock where we'd rescued the goat on Saturday afternoon. I wouldn't have recognised it if Aunty Wynn hadn't broken her silence in such a way that made me feel as if we were resuming a thread from one of the conversations of that day.

'I can certainly imagine it now,' she said.

'Imagine what?'

She shook her head. She was amazed that I didn't know what she was talking about. She leaned forward in her seat and squinted out the windscreen as if she were preparing to accelerate, to run something down.

'What it would be like to have locked-in syndrome,' she said.

I remembered the story she had told me Saturday.

'Can you imagine just lying there, watching your husband

or some other person going back and forth with the vacuum cleaner, and not being able to leave the room or even block your ears? I reckon I can. I bet he would do a rubbish job of it too. The vacuuming. I would certainly be able to tell.'

She glanced across at me then. She wanted me to know that I was the husband or some other person doing the inadequate job with the vacuum cleaner. In some ways so was my mother, and Stephen the vet, and maybe Bethany, and probably Uncle Cliff too. And Aunty Wynn was the one being forced to witness, powerlessly, and she would have liked nothing more than to close her eyes and block her ears and dissolve into that bed.

I'd moved to a very upright position. As I watched the road in front of us curve over and around those paddocks, I was trying to suppress an ill feeling that was rising to the top of my gut. I was aware of every mouthful of that biscuit swirling around inside me.

'If you had locked-in syndrome maybe your husband or some other person would prop you up before they did the vacuuming,' I said. 'So you could see what they were doing.'

'What difference would that make?' Aunty Wynn said.

'So you'd see that they were doing the best they could.'

'I can't say I'm sold on that.'

I cracked my window so I could hang my fingers out. The cold air made me feel better. I leaned back in my seat, closed my eyes and tried to think of stomach-calming things: dry crackers, ginger beer, apple boats, lying horizontal, a cold wet flannel to my forehead. I didn't blame Aunty Wynn for feeling like the butt of a very long, unfunny joke. I was more disappointed than anything else. Self-pity, this strange roundabout bitterness, wasn't what I'd come to expect—to need—from her.

'I just really'—I could hear her sucking her top teeth against her bottom lip, trying to hold something in—'I just really love the look of vacuum lines on a freshly vacuumed carpet.'

Her voice was full with a frightened, pre-emptive longing for something she had not yet lost.

'I know,' I said. 'Who doesn't.'

I woke alone to the sound of rain on the car roof. I'd left my cellphone at the house, so I didn't immediately know how long I'd been out—was it dusk or were the paddocks darkening because of heavy cloud? My left leg felt gammy and there was a sharp pain in my neck. My shoulders were aching too. I arched my body as best as I could in the confined space, extending my arms above my head and pointing my toes. And it did feel good, until I relaxed again. At which point I felt a lethargic wave surging through me. I want to describe it as sadness, but it was physical—moving through my limbs heavily. I felt so weighed down I was unsure whether I would be able to walk the short distance to the kitchen door.

I stayed in the car. I listened to the rain and didn't think about anything. Where would I have started? It was as if my whole system had finally overloaded, then crashed. Except it wasn't the kind of crash I'd been expecting—the spinning out of control, my wobbly spinning top. Maybe that had already happened. Now I was just blank. And heavy. Like a bag of wet sand.

How I ended up at Lia's house is still fuzzy.

I think a small part of me intended to confront Craig. Maybe to apologise. Did I hope that politely closing the door on that mess might keep the police from asking additional questions, or was I just expecting it would make me feel better? Or maybe I'd wanted to go over there to berate him for calling the police in the first place? I believe I could have gone either way. But I think the real reason I didn't head back into the house—even though the yellow kitchen lights made it look warm in there, full of good food smells, welcoming—was because I wasn't

ready to confront Aunty Wynn again, especially after what she had said to me in the car. And then there was my mother. So, when I eventually hauled myself out of the car, I headed down the driveway. Before long I was walking up Buttercup Green and turning into Freshfields Meadow. I almost made it to Craig's front door before I heard a familiar voice calling to me through the rain.

Maybe Lia just happened to be looking out her front window as I passed, though it was equally plausible that Aunty Wynn had noticed I was missing from the car and asked her to keep an eye out for me. Either way, I picture Lia framed by her large bay window, her face pressed to the cold glass, first curious, then concerned as her breath bloomed into her line of vision and she had to wipe it clear so she could get a clearer picture of me walking slowly and round- shouldered up the footpath in the cold and wet. If it had been me looking through that window instead of her, I would have pretended I hadn't seen and gone back to whatever I'd been doing. I wouldn't have had the energy or sympathy to deal with me.

'Erin!' she called, and she came bolting across the road carrying an umbrella.

For a stupid second I thought Lia was the police, coming to take me away for more questioning. Before I'd grasped what was happening, she had manoeuvred the umbrella over me and had her arm around my shoulders.

'You don't even have a raincoat on!'

'I'm okay,' I said, but I sounded feeble.

'You're soaked,' she said, squeezing me harder. 'Let's get you dry.' I saw her glance over my shoulder towards Craig's house. The expression on her face told me everything I needed to know about her dealings with the guy.

'I'm fine here,' I said. I wriggled out from under Lia's arm. It was the only attempt I made to stand my ground, to make out like I was in control.

'Let's get you dry, and then I'll drive you back to your aunty's. You don't have time to be sick with, gosh, pneumonia?'

Though it occurred to me later, and with some bitterness, that in a couple of days I would have plenty of time for an extended stay in hospital with pneumonia, I didn't argue with Lia again. In a flash we were standing inside her house.

It was warm and bright. I could smell bacon and something sweet and fruity. I was shivering. My clothes were soaked and I was already working on a puddle in the hallway. Lia ordered me to remove my shoes—Aunty Wynn's drenched orange submarines—and follow her into the bathroom. It was the kind of bathroom you would see in the 'after' shot in a TV ad for multipurpose cleaner. It was pristine. It put me at ease to be inside that bathroom. I took it all in: the hand-basin wide enough to sit inside, the ergonomic electric toothbrushes mounted on the wall, a pyramid of new toilet paper rolls on the cistern, thick eggshell-grey towels looped perfectly over the heated towel-rail, the plush thunderstorm-grey bathmat beneath my feet. I felt even better when the heat pump whirred into action and immediately started to warm the room. And then even better again when Lia turned on the shower and the space started to fill with steam.

'This is a really nice bathroom,' I said.

'I'll leave some dry clothes outside the door,' Lia said. 'And it's your lucky day—I just bought new undies.' She smiled warmly, patted my arm. 'So you don't need to go commando.' She pulled the door closed behind her.

I should have felt embarrassed then—alone, in that bathroom, listening to Lia leaving and then returning to place some clean clothes, including that brand new pair of undies, outside the door— but I didn't. Partly because of exhaustion. Also because it had been some time since anyone had taken care of me in this way, and I felt owed.

It took me longer than usual to get my jeans off. I rolled them

down my legs as if they were a wetsuit, tugging them only once they were at my ankles. I rolled my undies off the same way. My cardigan stank of wet sheep. I was happy to get my T-shirt and bra off, too. I hadn't changed since Saturday afternoon.

Once inside the shower, I turned to close the door behind me. It was a standard glass-box shower, though larger than most, and the glass door folded into four segments a bit like an accordion. As I grabbed the door by its chrome handle and attempted to pull it shut, my body suddenly went weak and I slipped backwards on my heels. This made me tug the door too hard, and it sprang out of its runner so half of it was free flying, swinging its way into the shower with me.

'What?' I said. I pushed the door back, trying to manoeuvre it into its track, but between the immense pressure of Lia's shower and how woozy I felt on bending over—the only thing I'd eaten all day was the biscuit Aunty Wynn had given me—I couldn't clearly see what I was doing.

'Shall I just leave it like this?' I asked no one.

I felt utterly useless. Instead of fighting that feeling and trying to hold it together—to hold the door together!—I leaned in to how completely and fully inept I felt. I gave the door a sharp, fed-up push. It jumped against its frame and swung right back to greet me.

'It's got a fucking mind of its own,' I said.

I started to cry—a pathetic, self-pitying sob. It didn't make me feel better. I wanted to break the door then. After the mortification of the day's events, and the unease of what tomorrow would bring, I think I just needed a win. It was me against those chrome and glass panels. I gave the door another sharp push, but with a lot more force this time, so it leapt back at me with a similar force and struck me in the face.

▲

The cut on the side of my nose only needed to be taped. Lia insisted that the one on my forehead would heal better with a couple of stitches. She had her home nurses' kit open and was messing around with skinny-nosed scissors and thread. I wasn't worried about the pain or whether or not I would have lasting scars. I was too distracted by how much blood I'd managed to spread around Lia's bathroom. From the dining room table where we were sitting, I could see one her bloodied towels where I'd left it on the floor of her kitchen. It was a disgusting article of uselessness. And I was its disgusting creator.

'Don't worry about the blood,' Lia said.

The cuts hadn't hurt while I was in the shower. The sight of all that diluted blood streaming down my sternum, over my breasts, hadn't affected the length of time I'd spent in there—I'd near poached myself. When I got out I could hardly stand up because I was so hot. And because of what had happened to my face—I hadn't been able to figure out the damage from the clouded bathroom mirror, which was why I'd dabbed at it so liberally with Lia's towel. My blood-sugar levels were also at rock bottom.

'Can I at least buy you some new towels?' I asked.

'Face wounds are the worst,' Lia said cheerfully, not objecting to my offer. She gently prodded at the cut on my forehead. 'This might sting. And I better get you another top.'

I looked down. The baby-blue polo shirt she had lent me had streaks of blood down the front and a little v-shaped sweat patch had appeared on the chest.

I'd never gotten stitches before. Lia was gentle, efficient. In the makeshift examination room that was her dining room, she was the perfect mix of friendly and professional. Although I felt better as I sipped on the Coke she had brought me, the faint started to scoot around my periphery again when she handed me a mirror.

'You're still looking a little peaky,' she said. 'Do you like bacon?'

I nodded sadly—the warm darkness sliding in, my wounds finally beginning to ache.

'I made devils on horseback,' she said. Her face lit up. 'My husband loves them, but he was called out on a job. I don't think he'll mind if we tuck in.'

'Sure,' I said, gulping back my soda—the sugar in combat with the determined faint.

'And if he does mind, too bad.' Lia stood up from the table.

Leaning back in my chair, still sweating profusely, I watched her move about her kitchen. The layout was similar but not identical to Bethany's and Craig's. It had the too-deep U-shaped counter with the inset oven and stovetop, double stainless-steel sink with one of those high looping taps, pale wood cabinets unblemished by handles, and the *like real marble* finish of the counter that Aunty Wynn had excitedly described for me on Saturday afternoon. The marble looked a lot like some kind of painted laminate. Lia had decorated the space nicely though. Each surface was appropriately adorned with new, brightly coloured enamel appliances, tea towels with zany prints, ceramic bowls with pictures of fruit on the side, full of actual fruit, and on the far wall I could see a giant framed 1960s advertisement for Marmite. It was safe kitsch, and all in balance—a kitchen in stark contrast to Craig's cat and tuna arrangement and Bethany's pileup of cheap booze. Adults lived here.

Lia returned with a plate of her bacon treats and a wad of paper towels. The delicious-smelling morsels held together with toothpicks were what I'd encountered when I'd first entered her house. We ate in silence for a bit. Though we were similar ages, Lia was streets ahead of me. I wondered if she thought that maybe I was just a woman in crisis, and that given an appropriate grieving period I would be back on track? Should

the police discover I had in fact stolen Craig's painting, and if I did end up back at the station, I hoped the person calling the shots might give me that same benefit of the doubt—I hoped they might also see I was a person to be pitied, pardoned.

'Why are they called devils on horseback?' I asked.

'I guess the devil is the bacon, and the horse is the prune,' Lia said.

'They're really good,' I said. Although I'd never previously enjoyed fruit that had been messed with (baked, stewed, jammed, dried, you name it), I'd already consumed my half of the plate. 'You have a nice place here.'

'The house I grew up in was tiny,' Lia said. 'There weren't many of us, but some days there wasn't enough oxygen to go around. I guess I always wanted a big house—big enough to swing a cat in each hand.' She laughed.

And I imagined Lia swinging those cats: Craig's cat was one.

'It can feel isolated on days like today,' she said. 'My family lives in Auckland, but it's a haul for them to get up here.' She sighed then, a sigh of both contentment and melancholy. She had what she wanted, but was it really what she wanted? She was still on the fence. 'So can you give me any good swimming tips?' she asked, brightening.

'Of course,' I said. 'What do you want to know?'

'Your aunty doesn't like to talk about swimming,' she said. 'Even when we're at the pool, swimming.'

I was slightly worried about the aftereffects of consuming so many prunes, though not enough to stop eating those bacon-wrapped gems. I was working my way through Lia's half now. 'What do you mean?' I asked her absently.

'She'll talk—as you know—about absolutely anything.' Lia gave me a look that suggested even she could tire of Aunty Wynn's one- sided rants. 'But actual swimming—real swimming, like what you do, what she did. The few times I've

asked her about it she looked really bummed out.'

I thought I saw a faint glint in Lia's eye then. I'd noticed that kind of sparkle before—from Aunty Wynn, when she was on the cusp of sharing some delicious gossip.

'My grandfather wouldn't let her go to the Commonwealth Games,' I said.

It wasn't delicious gossip—it was Aunty Wynn's life. She had been a sprinter—freestyle and butterfly—and she had been fast. One of her New Zealand records had remained unbroken for nearly twenty years. But when she qualified for the 1978 Games my grandfather wouldn't let her go—it would have taken her away from her farm obligations for too long. Now that I'd seen Aunty Wynn disappointed, hurt, I could picture that 'bummed out' expression, and it pulled at me.

'That could be something to do with it,' I said, surprised by my own candour.

I could tell Lia was trying to imagine Aunty Wynn as an athlete of real standing. Or maybe she was thinking about what she would do with this nugget of information, though I suspect it wasn't as juicy as she had hoped. She placed her hands flat on the table, gently drummed her fingers.

'All the ways our parents mess us up,' she said lightheartedly, singsongy.

'Yeah,' I said, though I wasn't thinking about my mother. 'I guess she must've given up trying to leave the farm after that.'

I'd prized Aunty Wynn's success when I was still swimming competitively. I never would have admitted it to her then, but I'd drawn strength from her wins—the potency of our shared athletic blood. I realised with a fresh urgency that I should admit that to her now. That it might be a small gift.

I was feeling more like myself. My energy was returning, but so was my fear of another sit-down with the police. Until I could find out what had happened and why I'd been allowed

to walk away, I knew that feeling would remain. And then I thought about my mother. Though I was dressed entirely in clothes that were not my own, and which I would never wear— baby pink sweatpants with *girl power* written in silver across the butt, that blood-streaked polo shirt, purple fluffy socks, Lia's surprisingly sexy undies—I was ready to get back to her. I'd last seen her only a few hours earlier, but I suddenly missed her powerfully. It was taking my breath away thinking about her now.

Lia must have seen it in my face. She lowered her voice, spoke gently: 'It'll get better.' She was looking at the sutured cut on my forehead, and then down across my nose—the exact imprint of a door punch to the face—but I knew she wasn't talking about that.

'Will it?' I asked, touching my hand to my head. I could feel those cuts throbbing perfectly.

'I took it back.'

Uncle Cliff was sitting at the kitchen table with half a dozen paper plates fanned out in front of him. Handfuls of small wet seeds of varying shapes were arranged on several of the plates. Next to the plates were as many jars—some containing a mucus-coloured pulp, others containing this same unpleasant-looking pulp but with red and pink bits floating on the top and at the bottom of the jar. His attention was focused on those seeds.

'I won't say the man's name,' he said, still not looking at me. He was skimming the top viscous layer of one of the jars with a spoon, then dumping the contents in a ceramic bowl. 'You know who I'm talking about.' His glasses were hanging on their bright yellow cord in the space between him and his vessels. I'd never actually seen those glasses on Uncle Cliff's face.

'What're you doing?' I asked. I was still trying to process what he had just said.

'These seeds are ready to start drying,' he said.

I dropped the plastic bag full of my wet clothes and shoes by the door, edged off the gumboots Lia had loaned me, and went to the fridge. I started taking Tupperware containers of Queen's Birthday lunch leftovers from the fridge and lining them up on the counter.

Uncle Cliff brought his newly skimmed jar to the kitchen counter too. 'I had a bad feeling when I saw you this morning,' he said. 'Then when I saw the police car pull up.' He poured the contents of the jar into a sieve that was sitting in the kitchen sink, then turned and looked at me. His expression was one of

disbelief then alarm. 'What happened there?'

My face was sore, and even more so now with his eyes on it. I could feel the depth of each wound. 'I got in a fight,' I said.

I could tell that Uncle Cliff was picturing me being pummelled by the man whose name he would not say. Inexplicably, I wanted him to believe that was what had happened, so I didn't correct him right away. I opened a few of the containers and inspected their contents—two and a half shell-less boiled eggs, some greyish chunks of chicken, and the remnants of Aunty Wynn's iceberg lettuce salad with Bethany's carrot matchsticks. The lids were all wet with condensation.

I explained what had happened at Lia's.

'That's where you've been,' Uncle Cliff said. Now he was running the tap through the sieve, rinsing the seeds. 'You were asleep in the car, and then you were gone.'

I nodded. I didn't have a reasonable explanation for just taking off.

'Anyhow,' he said, picking up his story, 'getting back the painting wasn't enough for that man—can you believe it? He still wanted to kick up a stink. So we had a little chat.'

I'd accepted that Uncle Cliff had probably been the one to move the painting from the bedroom cupboard where I'd stashed it, though I didn't know why or what had happened next. I hadn't imagined him confronting Craig.

'I told him that if he didn't fix the situation he'd put you in, I would tell the police everything I knew about the kind of man he was. He called them right then, didn't he?'

'They stopped questioning me pretty suddenly,' I said.

'Your cousin'll say she had it under control'—Uncle Cliff's voice sounded shaky—'but she's still just a silly kid.'

Despite the weird vibes I'd got from Craig and my unsettling interaction with him, I hadn't let myself seriously consider what Uncle Cliff was implying. Bethany wasn't yet seventeen. A year ago she would have been under the age of consent. I felt a cold

ripple down my spine, as if someone had dropped a handful of ice cubes down the back of my shirt. There was a dull ringing in my ears. I wished I could have felt disgusted and angry—as someone better than me would have. Instead, I found myself floored by a giant wave of relief. For getting away with what I'd done, yes, but also for what hadn't happened. What if Lia hadn't picked me up off the footpath? What if I'd knocked on Craig's door and instead of apologising or giving him a piece of my mind I'd let him take his dick out again? I also felt ashamed.

The tap was still running through that sieve of seeds, but Uncle Cliff wasn't paying it any attention. His eyes met mine and he visibly shuddered. 'Then I told him he should piss off.'

'Jesus,' I said.

I remembered how I'd first found Craig: floating in the pool, his arms extended, the cat sitting on his partially submerged chest. I'd too often confused the pull of desperation as a call to adventure. I had to stop pursuing men because I thought it would make for a good story. Especially as I didn't really have anyone to share all of these stories with.

'Jesus all right,' Uncle Cliff said.

'Erin, can I speak to you for a moment?' Aunty Wynn had joined us in the kitchen.

Uncle Cliff looked relieved to have finished his piece, and also like he wanted to be alone. He turned off the tap and patted me on the shoulder. Though I didn't deserve it, that little pat was immensely consoling.

'What the blazes happened to you? Your face.' Aunty Wynn was staring at me. Her hair had been washed and blow-dried into a broad frizzy halo.

Uncle Cliff unsnapped the kitchen door. 'I'll deal with those later,' he said, pointing at his freshly washed seeds. 'Oh and you'll be pleased to know the freesias look lovely.' Unsmiling, he hitched his shorts.

'When did you find the time to get banged up?' Aunty Wynn

said, once she was done waving Uncle Cliff out of the house.

I was scanning the kitchen pantry—I wanted bread, and to hide what I knew was written all over my face. On the bottom shelf of the cupboard I saw two stacks of sealed pallets of my mother's formula. Apocalypse food. I wondered what would happen to it when she was gone. Would Aunty Wynn donate it to another dying person? Or would it just sit there gathering dust? My mother would be ashamed of all of this—of everything I'd done, and of what had now been forced to the surface. What had happened between Bethany and Craig? And how did Uncle Cliff know about it? I hoped Bethany was okay. I also hoped she would never learn how her uncle had used her as leverage to save me.

'You haven't spoken to Lia?' I asked weakly.

'What about?'

I couldn't tell if Aunty Wynn had gotten over our earlier conversation about locked-in syndrome, or any of the other things that had happened in what had been a very long day. She seemed generally darker, like she might blow up at the slightest provocation, but also more open. More like my mother.

'I had an accident in her shower,' I said.

'What were you doing in her shower?'

All I could manage was a shrug.

Aunty Wynn was already standing within shaking distance of me. She reached out and cupped my chin. She turned my head from side to side, then gently peeled back a corner of the bandage on my forehead, squinted.

'She's done a nice job.'

She carefully patted the bandage back, and looked me square in the eye. She looked furious. It was different from the haughty kind of anger and frustration she had directed at me in the past. This was anger that had grown out of worry that had grown out of love. It had no veneer.

'What the blazes, Erin,' she said, as she started cleaning the

mess I'd left on the kitchen counter: a dirty butter knife, the open bread bag and Tupperware containers, a bed of crumbs where I'd made my sandwich before moving it to a plate.

When she was done, she turned and faced me again. She looked tired. She started to roll her shoulders in the way that was her habit—the nervous loosening of the upper body, just as she'd done Saturday afternoon in the paddock before she told me about my mother's plan to exit.

'Your mum wants to go to the beach tomorrow,' she said.

'The beach?' I said. 'Why?' I'd still not taken a bite from my sandwich, and instead was squashing it in my hands, playing it like it was a clarinet, unaware of what I was doing.

'She wants one last swim in the sea.'

Hanging on the hallway wall a few metres away was that old photo of Aunty Wynn and my mother dressed up in their surf-lifesaving gear. Remembering how they looked in that picture didn't make my mother's request for one last sea swim any less preposterous. Would we have to get her floaties for her arms? Maybe an inflatable tube to lie in? I pictured her poised on one of those inflatable pool loungers shaped like a flamingo or a slice of watermelon, a wind picking her up and whisking her out beyond our reach, so quickly that Aunty Wynn and I could do nothing but watch from the shallows.

'It's the middle of winter,' I said. 'She'll die of hypothermia.'

As I registered the absurdity of what I'd just said, Aunty Wynn and I exchanged a look that bordered on levity.

'I got her a wetsuit,' she said. I saw her mouth twitch with a smile.

I understood then why she had wanted to say all of this out of earshot of my mother, and possibly Uncle Cliff. They were innocuous things, not private, but, as I'd been for days, Aunty Wynn was a pinball machine of emotions. I think she was concerned that she might say something wrong, or something right but with the wrong tone, or that her face might reveal

how little she was holding it together. Because despite what had shifted between the two of us, it was everything to her that she remain upbeat, steady, silly ol' Auntyn Wynn for my mum.

'I also got us wetsuits,' she said. She couldn't believe what she was saying.

I was still kneading away at that sandwich with, I now realised, unwashed hands. The white triangles of bread had been compressed to reveal the lumps of chicken and egg inside. I'd already lost a crescent of boiled egg white to the floor. Although I didn't want to, I took a bite.

7

A year ago on Queen's Birthday Monday, the same year my mother was diagnosed, she and I sat at our kitchen table in Wellington while we were waiting for Aunty Wynn, Uncle Cliff and Bethany to arrive for the annual family lunch, and discussed how my mother wanted to be *laid to rest*. Though at that time there had been no way to tell whether she would live another year, or five, or more, she explained to me how she wanted her cremated remains scattered along Wellington's southern coast. She didn't mind which beach, but it would have to be secluded because she wanted there to be music and booze.

'I want to tell you these things while I can still talk,' she said. Her words had already begun to thicken and muddy. 'I'll give you money to buy a bottle of that champagne we had at your graduation.'

She called all carbonated wines *champagne*. The sparkling wine we'd had at my graduation dinner hadn't been; we'd found it on one of the bottom two shelves at the liquor store and it had cost twelve bucks.

'I guess I can do that,' I said.

It was cold that day, even for June. The electric heater had been wheeled beside the kitchen table where we were sitting in similar trackpants and hand-knitted woollen sweaters—my mother in what she called her 'eggplant muumuu', a baggy, thigh-length sweater in brownish-purple wool with flecks of yellow. There was a bacon quiche in the oven, and on the counter over my mother's shoulder was a gathering of fennel, celery, red onion and apple—the ingredients waiting to become

my disgusting fennel salad. My mother was holding a piece of toast slathered with honey in one hand and a mug of milky tea in the other. She took a bite of her toast, quickly followed by a gulp of tea. She had always eaten her breakfast that way, except now she had to lean down to her cup so she didn't have to lift it as far off the table. I watched her. Even then, I had a feeling that this was what I would miss most.

'If you buy it now and hide it in your closet,' she said, swallowing, 'you'll be ready.'

'I guess I could find a way to put some speakers in the back of your car,' I said, thinking about the musical element of her request. 'But, Mum, is that necessary?'

'I'd prefer to have the music playing as loud as possible.' She bobbed her head in time with the song playing on the kitchen radio. Her shoulder-length hair was held back in two faux-tortoiseshell combs—now one slipped, letting her hair fall around her face. 'I can't imagine us saying goodbye without some kind of soundtrack.'

I didn't like that my mother said 'us' when she spoke about the ceremony, as if she would be there, as if she would be more than a silent jar of burnt remains.

'Though I don't really want other people listening in,' she said, pulling the comb back through her hair and fastening it. 'It's not a free for all.'

When she said 'free for all' she slurred as if she were drunk. I'd mostly gotten used to her speech. I'd had to get used to it; we lived in different cities and we talked on the phone every few days. Then she would say something that was too slurred—too loose—for me to understand, and I'd been forced to accept those as real signs that she could be dead in just over a year.

'Mum,' I said, 'who made that?' I was looking at her eggplant-coloured sweater. It was unlike anything she had ever knitted. 'Did you?'

'God, I don't know,' she said. She looked down at herself,

inspected the sweater that was badly pilled after decades of wear and wash. 'Probably?'

It was the immaterial questions like this that made me acknowledge what my life would be like with my mother gone. If I couldn't ask *her* these things, then I couldn't ask anyone. The thought of not being able to get an immediate answer to this kind of question, and the small panic that ensued, was like having a drunken snog with my grief in the dark corner of a party—it was immediately followed by denial.

The way my mother sat at the kitchen table that morning revealed little of what her body was going through. She mostly looked her healthy fifty-five-year-old self, still commanding the room with the same self-assured posture that had scared so many of my friends. 'It's my shoulders that make me seem intimidating,' she liked to say, usually when she got her way at the post office or the bank. Her beautiful broad shoulders. Though she wasn't the sort of mother who radiated warmth either.

'Whatever happens'—she was talking about the ceremony again—'my sister and brother don't get a say, whatever they tell you. Especially you know who.'

'What if they want to be there?' I asked. 'When I scatter the ashes.'

'Then do it before they can organise to fly down.'

I doubted this would be possible, but I nodded.

'I don't mind whether you drink the champagne before or after you scatter me,' she said.

'I'll probably have to drink the bottle of wine before I do it,' I said.

She picked up her empty plate with two hands then placed it back on the table. She looked shaken, though there were no tears in her eyes—she looked as if she were about to laugh. 'Shit it,' she said.

Then she did laugh. It was an awful, hacking laugh that came

from a place of fear, not joy. She stood and shuffled across the floor to the kitchen sink, holding her plate out in front of her like an offering. She placed it on the counter with a rattle. She had been having trouble putting on and taking off her shoes, and her feet were unreliable without a solid platform and Achilles support, so I'd bought her a pair of Crocs. She turned around and looked at me, then she glanced down at her feet—giant and clown-like in those plastic purple shoes—as if there were answers to be found there.

Out the window behind her was our small backyard rimmed with bare pōhutukawa. The lawn, well overdue for a mow, was covered in dandelions, and the vegetable garden had gone to seed. I could see one sparrow on the bird feeder, its feathers ruffled against the cold.

'In that case,' she said, 'I'll give you money for two bottles.'

I'd been going through the motions. During that conversation, and for too long after. I hadn't really believed that she wanted me to do those things, or that I would need to do them. If I had believed it, I couldn't imagine carrying them out. My mother in an urn! My mother flying in the wind! While I was drunk on the most gaseous sparkling wine! What if bits of her flew into my hair?

But here we almost were.

Despite what Uncle Cliff had said, the freesias looked insane. My mother's room was bursting with vases, jars, even a couple of old tin cans crammed with bunches of the flowers. Uncle Cliff's guy had outdone himself. The scent was sweet but overpowering. While I was gone, someone had shown my mother how to play the music on my phone through the small panda bear speaker. I could hear sad guitar music that conjured up images of bra-less women in long muslin dresses, and that, paired with the flowers, made me feel like I'd entered

the viewing room before the funeral, to pay my mother one last visit before she was sealed up in her coffin, on her journey to the urn. Except she wasn't dead or even lying supine. She was sitting propped up in her kimono with some multi-coloured beads around her neck, busy fiddling with medical equipment. She looked up from what she was doing and gave a limp-armed sweep of the room like a pleased but tired gameshow host. Then she frowned as she saw my face. I could see that the clothes I was wearing—Lia's clothes—confused her too.

'I wanted to look nice for tomorrow,' I said.

I was still reeling from Uncle Cliff's confession. My feelings of guilt were growing, and I didn't feel anything like true relief, but something was easing in me. I'd started to feel a small reassurance in knowing that my troubles had company. My mother, Aunty Wynn, now Uncle Cliff, and, in some ways, Bethany—they were all, in one way or other, caught up in the things I was caught up in. It was a selfish comfort, but it was enough for me to feel lightened. My mother didn't chuckle at my remark as I'd hoped, though—she looked upset. Her iPad was sitting nearby, and after I told her an abbreviated version of the shower-door-to-the-face story, I waited for her to ask about my afternoon at the police station. I figured she must have prepared a note about her concerns, her relief, even a simple telling-off? Instead, she motioned for me to move closer.

I scooted up the bed with the last of my sandwich on a plate in my lap. She attempted to cup my chin as Aunty Wynn had, then instead indicated I should move closer. She peered at my face, the way only a mother can: with a determined sense of ownership. Though I was twenty-six years old, my face was still her face to inspect. She didn't like what she saw, but it wasn't life-threatening. She dropped her eyes and went back to what she was doing.

On the tray in front of her was an empty glass vial, its metal cap peeled back to reveal its rubber stopper. There was a large

plastic feeding syringe connected to a length of tubing that ended in a port, like the feeding tube that had been implanted in her stomach, and a smaller syringe and a plastic cup. I knew exactly what she was up to. She was practising the steps she would have to complete tomorrow evening—everything she would need to do to take her own life, without assistance, so her family would be in the clear and it would seem, from a doctor's point of view, that there was no need for an autopsy, because she had simply died in her sleep from respiratory failure, as was expected of her.

The real vial of Nembutal was sitting on her bedside table. Someone—maybe my mother, though more likely Aunty Wynn—had already peeled back the perforated circle in the middle of the metal seal, so the soft rubber stopper was exposed. The vial was ready and waiting.

I'd read stories about people with terminal illnesses who were prepared to take their own lives, but once they acquired the means to do so they no longer felt the need. All they had wanted was a safety net for when it got too scary up there, on the every-single-day tightrope walk of not dying. I hadn't thought this would be the case with my mother, and here was the last bit of proof. Even with the aid of one of Aunty Wynn's special tools, she wouldn't be able to remove the entire metal seal or rubber stopper from the vial, at least not without spilling its contents, so before anything else she would have to extract the drugs via the syringe. It wasn't complicated—anyone who had the fine use of their hands could complete the task with ease. But my mother?

She was taking a long, shaky time with each step. Even with nothing but air inside, the syringe provided too much resistance, and she could only draw it out part way. Watching her was like watching a toddler trying to cram a triangle block into a triangular hole at the wrong angle. Her motor functions seemed to have declined even during the time I'd been visiting.

Yet her determination was clear. This was happening.

'I hear we're going to the beach tomorrow?' I said.

She looked up briefly, nodded. As she manoeuvred the equipment in her hands, she brushed the front of her kimono, revealing the clamped end of her feeding tube.

When she first got a feeding device, she had her old in-home nurse hook it up to a bag full of blue Gatorade. She had never consumed a sports drink before, but on learning that they were one of the liquids she could ingest through her tube she couldn't resist. Together we'd watched as that unreal blue liquid travelled down the tube and vanished into her gut. We'd both chuckled, then I'd felt mortified. But that was nothing. Not now.

The air was thick with the scent from the freesias and I was starting to feel overwhelmed. I rubbed my neck, convinced that my throat might be starting to close up. When I delivered a dry, pathetic cough my mother looked up again.

'Why freesias?' I asked.

She placed everything back on the tray and pushed it to the side.

I waited while she typed her reply.

PAINTIMG

'Uncle Cliff sorted it out,' I said.

She looked as if she already knew this. That's not what she was asking.

'It was a dumb mistake,' I said. This was true, but how could I also tell her everything that painting represented for me? 'I got carried away.'

She wasn't satisfied. She wanted to know everything, all the details of how and why I'd stolen that painting, but we were running out of time. There was something else she needed me to read. She turned the iPad to face me.

I DON'T HAVE ANY LAST WORDS OF WISDOM FOR YOU. SORRY, LOVE. LIFE'S FUNNY. YOU'RE FIGURING IT OUT.

I tried to scroll down to see if she had written anything else. She hadn't. I'd not thought much about how we would say goodbye, what our last *moment* would look like—I'd been dreading it and it wasn't something I'd wanted to think about. However, I hadn't expected this: so soon, and so little.

I placed my hands in my lap and sat dead still. I felt stiff and at the same time like a fistful of cooked spaghetti held together with a single elastic band. I couldn't figure out if I was angry. Did I feel let down? Did I feel sad? Did I feel lonely? Did I feel that my mother not giving me advice was her weird way of giving me advice? Did I get that yet? Or did I want to throw a tantrum?

'I wouldn't say I was figuring it out,' I said finally.

My mother looked bugged by my response. She was holding the large feeding syringe, the one that would be connected to her feeding tube, with nowhere near enough height and at too obtuse an angle.

Then she looked saddened.

Then she looked terrified.

I wanted to ask her questions. Big questions, like: Will I be okay? Should I give up on trying to be a curator? Do I really have the heart of a thief? And smaller questions, like: Does my new hair colour actually suit me? How much vitamin D is the correct amount? Do I eat enough fish? Can I wear the colour yellow now? Is there a trick to cleaning gutters? What do I do if the washing machine floods? Where's the recipe for your bacon quiche?

I wanted to ask all of these things and to take extensive notes. Even if I then discarded those notes—my mother's advice—and fumbled my way through on my own, I wanted the luxury of being able to choose. The gift of being able not to listen. Though how was I supposed to begin asking what I wanted to know? The song playing through Bethany's panda had finished and, except for the frustrated rattle of my mother dropping the

plastic equipment back on the tray, the room was quiet.

Watching her repeat those simple excruciating tasks reminded me of how I'd used to feel the night before a big swimming race, with a thick worry in the pit of my stomach, which, with all the training and preparation done, I would try to ease with sit-ups. I would lie in the living room with a bunch of couch cushions beneath me and do hundreds of them. I would count out each number at the top of my lungs till I felt the right amount of tired and psyched. Maybe my mother was doing something similar—calming herself by practising, by making the actions feel familiar, by seeing how she could best not spill the drugs, how she could do it all efficiently.

As I watched her renew her struggle to keep the large feeding syringe upright while she unclamped the feeding tube, the unclamping that would allow the Nembutal to travel into her stomach already coated with anti-nausea medication, I had another thought: she wanted me to witness her struggling.

Because she wanted me to see that she might not—would not—be able to do it. So I could prepare myself. Not for her failure, but so I would be ready to step in and finish it for her.

Tuesday

I put my wetsuit on beside the car so I would have less to carry. It was short in the legs and arms, unlike the full-length varieties Aunty Wynn had acquired for herself and my mother, and roomy in the boobs and butt, where it ballooned, making me look much curvier than I was. It was obviously secondhand, and it had aged to a dry elephant grey all over except for the pink panels down the thighs and back that were their original hot pink near the seams but faded to the colour of pork sausages in the centre. Across the chest were the remnants of an illegible logo—now just flaky scabs of violet.

It was a cold, rainy day, exactly what you would expect for June. Though the rain had eased to overcast by the time we arrived at the beach, our car was the only one in the car park. We walked along the track that wove through the sand dunes to the beach. As we emerged from the dunes I saw that we would be the only people on the beach too.

The tide was halfway out. And there was something wrong with the water. It was meant to be a surf beach—the kind where fishermen got thrown and bloodied against the rocks at the south end and where swimmers drowned all the time; the kind where there were no sharks because they don't like it rough—but the water was calm and smooth, with only a couple of tiny waves sloshing against the black sand.

'I thought it was a surf beach,' I said.

I was carrying the picnic hamper in one hand and slowly guiding my mother and her walker along the sand with the

other. Beside us, Bethany was carrying all of the beach chairs.

'It is,' Aunty Wynn said, amazed. 'Look at it, Helen.'

My mother looked at it with a grim expression.

She didn't fill out her wetsuit very well either. Her inadequacies were similar to mine, but more pronounced because her wetsuit covered her whole body except for her hands, feet and head. We'd helped her put it on at the house. She didn't have a pair of togs, so she was wearing a stretched-out, chlorine-bleached pair belonging to Aunty Wynn, which had gone on after Aunty Wynn had disconnected my mother's feeding tube and carefully plugged up the hole. Aunty Wynn and I then had the task of rolling the legs of the suit up my mother's legs, hoisting the back up over her tiny butt, feeding her arms into each sleeve, and zipping it all up. It was the first time my mother had let me help dress her. I'd expected it to be mortifying, extremely awkward—the zipper, with its long cotton tab, making me think of some kind of futuristic funeral shroud—but my mother had laughed the whole time. She was in an extraordinarily happy mood. And that had put me in a tentatively okay mood. Once suited up, she put her kimono on over the top and Aunty Wynn helped her into a pair of sneakers.

Now Aunty Wynn was inspecting the sky above her. 'It's an easterly,' she said. 'A bloody easterly.'

'How do you know?' I asked.

'Elementary meteorology, Erin,' she said. 'Gosh, I bet that's one beauty of a high pressure system.' She shook her head with pleasure.

'Jeez, where are the waves?' Bethany said. She let the beach chairs she'd been carrying drop in a heap on the sand. Bethany had been a last-minute addition to our trio, having managed to wrangle a day off school out of her mother.

'It's flat as a pancake,' Aunty Wynn said.

'How am I going to do any body surfing?' Bethany said. She was wearing enormous sixties-style sunglasses with amber-tinted lenses. Her face was swimming behind them.

'We might as well have gone to the pool,' I said.

My mother grunted her disappointment too. When she had pictured her last swim in the sea, it hadn't looked like this.

'I want you to put this on,' Aunty Wynn said. She was holding something that looked like a balaclava made out of rubber.

Aunty Wynn looked amazing in her wetsuit. It was a sleek near- black that hugged her body so convincingly, so perfectly smoothed her out, that she looked like a big beautiful auburn-haired sea lion. She had put it on back at the house and driven to the beach wearing nothing else.

'It'll keep your head warm, Helen,' Aunty Wynn said. 'Stop the heat escaping.'

My mother gave Aunty Wynn a thumbs down. She wasn't interested in keeping her head warm. Not today. She wanted to feel as much of that chilled salty air as possible. She was sitting in a folding chair, the kind that is very upright and looks as if it might snap back into its folded position at any moment. She had a wool blanket across her lap and was staring out to sea with the most puzzled expression. Her walker was within reach—its four wheels were surprisingly good on the sand, as if the manufacturer had foreseen final off-road trips such as this.

'Look, I'll put mine on first,' Aunty Wynn said. She spoke with the kind of false enthusiasm that a parent might use when trying to convince a child to eat their broccoli.

When she was done, a few strong curls of auburn hair poked through the visor. She hadn't removed her glasses, which sat crookedly on her face, but otherwise the image of Aunty Wynn the sea lion was complete. The queen of the sea lions. A regal and ridiculous ball of nervous energy.

She had been antsy all morning, and she had been channelling that energy into a violent enthusiasm. On our drive to the beach she had played a CD of Irish folk songs—retrieved from a CD wallet that she had stashed on her side of the car—while she and my mother sang and hummed along badly. Before I'd seen her final wish list, I'd never once heard my mother mention Irish folk songs. And yet there she was, doing her best to mouth and hum the words of a CD full of them. It was the last day of her life, and the list of things I would never share with her—the things I would never *get*—was still growing.

'I'm going in,' Aunty Wynn said. 'Helen, you too? Erin? Bethany?'

My mother gestured to me to remove the blanket from her lap.

Bethany ignored her mother. She was already down to a purple and yellow terry-cloth bikini and was stretched out on the full-length beach lounger my mother had been reclining on the day before. Her body looked grey-blue in the milky winter light. Though there wasn't anyone on the beach to impress, it also being a weekday and no longer a public holiday, she flat out refused to wear a wetsuit. Hers was the sister suit to mine, with yellow panels where I had pink.

I'd wanted to talk to her since my conversation with Uncle Cliff the previous evening. Uncle Cliff had used what had happened between her and Craig as leverage to get me off the hook. I hadn't objected, and I don't think Aunty Wynn knew about any of it, otherwise I doubt she would have let Bethany continue to stay in that house on her own. We were all failing her. As her older cousin, her older cousin who knew, I needed to do better.

'Bethany, you coming in?' I asked, folding the blanket and placing it on top of my chair.

She had her earbuds in and was plugged into her iPhone, though she must have heard me because from behind those

amber lenses she opened her eyes to slits. In the car, she had wanted to know what had happened at the police station. I'd only given her a vague account: 'They asked me some questions, it was nothing.' She had also asked about the bandages on my forehead and nose, to which I'd responded, 'I lost a boxing match with a shower door.' She had rolled her eyes at that. Now she inspected me with scepticism. I could see goosebumps on her legs and arms.

'Want me to get your wetsuit?' I asked.

'Nah,' she said, closing her eyes, returning to her own thoughts, or to John, or Paul, or Neil, or Jim. 'I'm good for now.'

'She's fine,' Aunty Wynn said.

'Okay,' I said, raising my hands defensively.

I was already feeling the effects of the cold in my mid-length wetsuit, and started to shiver. Even though I had no intention of putting my face in the water—my cuts were still ripe—I wanted another layer to protect my ears. I wanted to more comfortably join my mother in the water, to share in her final request, and to be nearby in case anything went wrong. 'Is there a hood for me?' I asked.

Aunty Wynn glanced at me and started rummaging around in her bag, pretending to look for something that I was pretty certain wasn't there. She carried on talking to my mother, telling her a story about a patient at the diagnostic clinic where she worked who had recently vacationed in Italy. The woman had travelled as part of a tour group for, what Aunty Wynn described as 'older independent ladies'. 'I don't see why I couldn't do that,' she was saying. 'I've always wanted to visit Pompeii, where those poor souls were buried by that volcano. Who knows why?'

I'd started to shiver. When Aunty Wynn had acquired our wetsuits, she had made a judgement about me. I had not, in her mind, earned the right to wear a full-length suit. Or even

one that fitted me properly. In addition to its other flaws, my wetsuit was too narrow across the shoulders and I had to keep the zipper partly undone so the collar wouldn't choke me. Half my back was exposed. 'When did you get these?' I asked Aunty Wynn, interrupting again. 'The suits?'

It was a small, silly question, but I needed—*craved*—further confirmation that I was ready for all this stuff, for what I would face with my mother later that night, and then what I would face without my mother after it was all over. I was also scared about what it meant if I *was* ready to face this stuff, what it would mean about the kind of person I would be once I'd helped my mother take her own life. In that moment, Aunty Wynn's opinion about the kind of wetsuit I was allowed to wear, knowing *when* she had decided not to spend the extra money on the second half of the sleeves and legs, the extra rolls of fabric that would have put me on par with her and my mother, in their mini club, seemed like an important gauge of these things.

'I don't really remember,' Aunty Wynn said. She tossed me the hood my mother had turned down. 'If your mum doesn't want it.'

I examined the hood—the faceless head and neck of a dummy— as she made herself busy helping my mother out of her shoes and kimono then assisting her with her walker. In no time at all, they were out of earshot, heading towards the water's edge.

'Did you get one of these?' I asked Bethany. I sounded pathetic, like a kid on the verge of tears.

Bethany removed her earbuds this time and propped herself up on her elbows. She looked mystified. 'Screw it,' she said.

I watched as she got up from the lounger and took off down the beach towards the sea, her lovely hippy body bursting out of the purple and yellow bikini with every long and surprisingly

graceful stride. Overtaking my mother and Aunty Wynn, she was the first to hit the water—with a splash and a string of curse words—then she bellyflopped onto the first tiny wave that came her way.

I ventured in to above my knees, just deep enough for the water to creep in under the hem of my wetsuit. It was absolutely freezing. It was excruciating to be in. My mother and Aunty Wynn were much further out, my mother having decided, once she was submerged, that she didn't mind that there were no waves. The two of them were laughing, the water up to their ribs. From where I was standing, my mother—so well supported by the salt water, Aunty Wynn's extended helping hands mostly concealed—almost looked her old, healthy self. After a few more bellyflops, Bethany left the exposed part of the beach and disappeared into the sand dunes with her towel.

Aunty Wynn was still loudly talking about her future tour of Italy. 'I also want to go to Venice. Can you imagine living above all of that water?'

I could tell my mother was only part listening. Her head was pitched back and her eyes were open to the matt grey sky. Now I could clearly see Aunty Wynn's arms supporting her around her middle. I hadn't put on the hood, and I was swiftly reaching the limit of how much cold I could handle, my teeth chattering so hard my jaw was starting to ache.

'I would love to ride in one of those, what are they called? Gondolas?' Aunty Wynn said. 'Do you think that's a good idea?'

If my mother gave some kind of response, I couldn't see or hear it. She continued to lean back, stare at the sky.

Two sisters, somewhat together.

'I think I could do that,' Aunty Wynn said to herself.

My mother floated to an upright position then. She turned to face me and lifted her arm slightly out of the water.

I waved back. 'You good?'

My mother grinned and flipped me something like the bird. A mother and daughter, also somewhat together.

I could see that my mother and Aunty Wynn would be a while, so I followed the sand avalanche Bethany had created and found her on the other side of the dune's first hump, nestled in some dune grass. She was lying on her stomach on a towel, her hands and feet burrowed into the sand, her bikini bottoms riding up her butt.

'Hey,' I said, as I skied my way down to join her.

She was still wearing those monstrous sunglasses. She didn't seem surprised to see me. 'Hey,' she said.

There was no breeze in that hollow, though the sand was still unpleasantly damp.

'It's definitely warmer in here,' I said, parking myself at the foot of the dune. 'Aren't you cold though?'

She clearly hadn't dried herself before rolling around in the sand. Her pale skin was covered in blotches of shimmering black. Her wet hair was caked in it too.

'I don't really get cold,' she said.

I tried not to stare at the goosebumps on her arms and back. 'I think our mums are going to be a while.'

Rolling over and raising herself up on her elbows, she sighed. 'Is there something specific you'd like to talk about?' She said this warily, as if she were an underpaid and underappreciated public health therapist.

'In many ways you're just like your mum,' I said. 'In other ways you're completely different.'

'That's usually how it goes,' she said. Nothing about her body language gave anything away about which part of herself—the part that was like Aunty Wynn, or the part that wasn't—she liked most.

'I heard something about you and Craig,' I said.

She narrowed her eyes. 'What did you hear?'

'Enough to wonder if you were okay.'

A long silence followed. I could see her trying to figure out how much she wanted to share, weighing how much she trusted me against how much of her guard she was willing to let down. She started rolling one corner of her towel up into a little spring roll, unrolling it, rolling it up again. The longer I waited, the more nervous I became about what she might end up sharing.

'You want to know something cool?' she said eventually.

I was crouching with my back to the sand dune. Even though the zipper of my wetsuit was completely undone, the posture made the fabric strain against my throat. I rolled the wetsuit partway off my shoulders—feeling colder, but freer.

'Sure,' I said.

'I might be getting a part-time job working on a free-range chicken farm.'

'Instead of working at the vets?' I said.

'Nah,' she said, sitting up straight now, her legs crossed. 'As well as. They're organic free-range actually. I'm not super interested in working with birds, or with farm animals really, but it'll be a good experience. I'll probably have to do a lot of cleaning, and feed the chickens, and maybe learn how to give them health checks. If that's required.'

I couldn't imagine being so enthusiastic about cleaning up after, feeding, touching or even being around chickens, but this was what kept Bethany going. These jobs were all steps towards her realising her dream of working with some kind of cute zoo animal. In this way we were no different—both of us plumping up our resumes while hoping to meet the person who would give us our breaks. If she hadn't already done so, at some point she would probably encounter the veterinary version of Karl and Mean Space. I hoped she would make better choices than me.

'I've already met the chickens,' she said. 'They're what's called a dual-purpose breed because they're good for eggs and meat.'

'I'm surprised you're not a vegetarian,' I said.

'Why?' Bethany said. She was clearly frustrated by this comment. 'Chickens are bred to be eaten, and cows, pigs, lambs—that's a dumb thing to say. You should see these birds though. They have these super cute black and white feathers.'

I could picture those chickens, but it did nothing for me.

Bethany was laughing to herself now. 'Chickens are pretty stupid,' she said. Then in a flash she straightened up, feeling guilt maybe that she had criticised the feathered pals who would help her get what she wanted.

'We can't all be pygmy marmosets,' I said.

She seemed pleased that I'd remembered the name of her dream animal. She reached back and rolled and then unrolled the corner of her towel one last time, spread it out, patted it flat with her hand. 'He said I was getting fat,' she said. 'Craig.'

I had no trouble imagining Craig saying this. The shame I'd felt the day before rose to the surface again. 'What a dick.'

She nodded. 'I told you he's a dick.'

In the brief silence that followed, I heard Aunty Wynn call my name. The dog-whistle she had used to fetch me from the car on Saturday afternoon followed. Bethany rolled her eyes, irritated that her mother was interrupting us at this turn in the road. She also seemed resigned, too resigned for someone so young.

'You'd better go,' she said. 'Mum's got her whistle on.'

'I don't have to,' I said.

She leaned back on her elbows, stretched out her legs. 'Yeah you do.'

I'd wanted her to confide in me about Craig—partly for selfish reasons, to alleviate some of my guilt, but also because I wanted to try and do right by her, having squandered every other opportunity. Although something about the way she

looked at me from behind those sunglasses suggested she had little interest in confiding—not in the way I wanted. No, despite her age, and how her braces, bright with saliva, twinkled as she half-smiled, I think she might simply have wanted to talk to me as an equal: as a woman who had been let down by a man, to a woman who had very likely also been let down by a man. I thought she looked a lot like how I'd felt after getting off the phone to Karl on Sunday night.

Aunty Wynn was continuing to call my name and whistle. I reluctantly started my retreat up the sand dune, then stopped halfway and turned to face Bethany. She was watching me go.

'I wish I could hurt that guy for you,' I said.

'Yeah, thanks,' she said.

We would have many more opportunities, but she would never completely confide in me about what had happened between her and Craig. I wouldn't even learn the details of how long it had lasted, so I could never know how much consent she had been able to give. Yet what kind of leverage would Uncle Cliff have had if there was no question about this? The round, hard fears we carry with us.

The last time I swam in a New Zealand championship race I'd bombed out. Badly. I'd felt terrible in the water—tired and heavy, as if I had sandbags tied to my hands and feet. At the time, I blamed my coach for not properly tapering me and giving me enough rest. It wasn't that simple though.

I'd gone to primary school with a kid who was a middling whizz on the violin. At nine years old he was already sick of it. Instead of telling his parents he wanted to quit, he ollied his skateboard onto the violin and bow on the netball courts during lunchbreak, hoping, I guess, that his parents wouldn't be able to afford a new instrument and he would be off the

hook. Swimming and I were something like that. Except, I was the kid as well as the violin and bow.

I remember sitting on the edge of the warm-down pool after that last race. Not yet ready to admit that it would be my last race, I simply felt like a failure. I looked up into the stands where my mother was sitting with her knitting, stop-watch, pages of notes, final times and splits, expecting her to look angry—all that time and energy, all of those early morning starts and late nights, the weekends spent travelling for meets, not to mention the money, wasted. She did look frustrated, and a familiar ill feeling rose to the top of my gut. Then her face softened. She leaned forward in her seat and mouthed: *Let's get the fuck outta here*, throwing a thumb over her shoulder at the end, so there was no way for me to misunderstand.

She was able to save me with a curse word and thumb jerk. Now, as I reached the top of the sand dune, I saw Aunty Wynn helping her out of the water and back to her walker. I skidded-ran the rest of the way down the dune, and sped down the beach to her side. My mother didn't need my assistance though—she was happy moving at her own pace to where our chairs were arranged in a crescent around the picnic hamper. Not yet satiated, Aunty Wynn headed straight back into the water.

'Do you want me to help you out of the wetsuit?' I asked.

Sitting in her chair with one towel around her shoulders, another wrapped around her head, she looked cold. Her lips were bright red and her cheeks were pink, but she shook her head. She wanted the moment to last a little longer. Even without any waves, even in the cold, being there was life giving for her and Aunty Wynn, and maybe Bethany, in a way that none of it was for me. I didn't feel envious though. No, it was the first time I was able to properly picture my mother and Aunty Wynn as the Moore Sisters, ruling the pool, ruling the

beach, carefree and confident. In spite of the obvious things that hadn't worked out, at least my mother had chosen her life. And maybe it had been a good life.

Aunty Wynn stopped swimming. She waved at us from the water.

'Can you believe this?' she yelled at the top of her lungs, gesturing all around her.

I waved back.

My mother presented a tired thumbs up to no one in particular.

Once Aunty Wynn had given my mother the precautionary anti-nausea medication, she left the two of us alone. I sat cross-legged on the end of my mother's bed. It turned out that the old TV she had brought with her from Wellington actually worked, and we were watching *Dancing with the Stars*—a show neither of us had watched before. She was dressed in her nightie and kimono. The yellow and green seventies-style dress was on a hanger behind her bedroom door. That was where it would remain, at least till I left the Moore family house a couple of weeks later.

'I've never really got dancing,' I said. 'As a vocation.'

All the enthusiasm and verve my mother had displayed at the beach, and the calm and contentment that had followed on the drive home, had been replaced by a profound tiredness. If earlier in the day I'd had any doubts about whether she was ready to let go, I understood then that it had taken the last of her remaining energy stores to be anyone close to the woman she recognised as herself that afternoon. Now she'd had that, she had already started to let go.

'Do you remember the time you took me to the ballet?' I said. 'You let me eat an entire family-size bag of Minties.'

She turned away from the TV long enough to give me a look that said 'As if'.

'By the time the ballet was finished, my jaw was so sore. Now I can't smell mint without my jaw sending out warning signals.' I opened and closed my mouth to stretch my jaw muscles.

She gestured to me to hand her the iPad. She took a long time typing her response, long enough for the couple on the TV to be given their feedback and scores, and for the show to cut to a commercial break. There was an ad for Toilet Duck, one for some kind of healthy protein bar, and then there appeared the same shot of the same dog on the back of the same 4WD motorbike herding the same cows that my mother and I had thought, on Saturday night when we'd seen it first, was a farming show but had turned out to be an ad for dog food.

My mother pushed the iPad towards me and then turned her attention to the TV. She had always loved dogs. She'd had a farm dog, a border collie like the one on TV, when she was a kid. We watched the commercial in silence, with an interest neither of us had had on Saturday night, until the jangly country music reached its crescendo and the guy on the motorbike turned around and violently hugged the ecstatic border collie, as the brand of dog food superimposed itself over them both. I couldn't remember the last time anyone had hugged me like that. My mother seemed to be in a trance. Was she thinking about all the years of dogs she could have had if it weren't for my allergies? Was she, too, wondering about the last time someone had hugged her that way?

I wanted so much to scoot up the bed then, to reach out and scoop her up in a powerful hug—to breathe in her warm, dying mother smells, to squeeze her with all my strength. But I didn't. I couldn't. We were who we were. I am who I am. Instead we sat in silence, cuddling our own thoughts, and I didn't want her

to see how I had started to cry so I sat facing the TV, unmoving for a long while.

When I did finally turn around, my face dry, I saw the iPad screen.

WE=BAD TEETJH

This wasn't an enlightening observation. I had a mouth full of fillings, and earlier that year I'd received my second root canal. 'I know, Mum,' I said.

She didn't respond. She pulled back the blanket to reveal her feeding tube, prepped and ready. She began to extract the Nembutal from its vial. I sat motionless for a few seconds, taking in everything that was happening. I was afraid to move in case I shook the bed and made my mother spill something or drop something. The realisation that the last conversation I would have with her was about our inferior teeth genes descended on me like a swift-moving fog. It numbed me, blotted me out, but there wasn't time to try for something better.

My mother didn't look at me—she was concentrating all of her strength on those few, light medical pieces. Though, even with the vial of Nembutal only partly drained, I could see she was unable to go on. It was too hard. She didn't have the physical strength. She still wouldn't look me in the eye—she sat motionless, as motionless as she could, both of her hands gripping a container. Without saying anything, I unfolded my legs, slid off the bed, leaned over and took what was in her hands into mine.

'This goes here, right?' I said.

She did her best nod.

The gin and tonic she had requested—the final item on her list— was sitting on her bedside table, untouched, in a pool of condensation.

'Then in here?' I said.

My mother just stared at me. A smile twitched at the corner of her mouth.

'This next?' I asked, pointing at the clamp.

The expression in my mother's tired, swamp-coloured eyes told me everything I needed to know.

I unclamped her feeding tube. It was something I'd seen Aunty Wynn do multiple times. It wasn't complicated—it was like a peg you might use to keep an opened bag of cornflakes fresh. After that I picked up the water flush, which was also sitting on the bedside table.

Most of the Nembutal had already gone.

It was then that I heard the sound of Aunty Wynn's Ugg boots shuffling along the hallway. She appeared in the doorway, stony-faced, dressed in her old lady's nightie, a cup of tea in her hand. I didn't wait for her to come in and take over, and there was something about the way she stood just outside the bedroom door that told me she wouldn't.

'Just a little will do,' she said, nodding at the container of water.

I quickly poured out a mouthful of water, ensuring that the rest of that clear liquid, which from a distance could also have been water, but wasn't, made it down the tube and into the hole in my mother's stomach. As soon as it was all gone, I wished with every cell in my body that I could suck it back out.

While all of this was happening, my mother didn't take her eyes off me.

Until she could no longer keep her eyes open.

As she lost consciousness I became aware of the jazzy pop music that was playing on the TV. It was the backing track for the next dance routine: 'Blame it on the Boogie'. It was only then that I remembered Bethany's Bluetooth panda, silently watching us from the shelf. When I consider all of the failures of my life—up until that point, at twenty-six, standing at my mother's bedside, and then the new failures I've racked up in the few years since—that remains one I can't shake, one I can't excuse. It niggles at me, burrowing, like a soft brown worm

working its way through a piece of fruit. The list of songs my mother had wanted to hear for her final frolic had completely slipped my mind. Instead, I was letting her die to 'Blame it on the Boogie'.

I was too scared to move from her side to turn off the TV. Aunty Wynn remained hovering in the doorway. We bore it out together. The contestants finally completed their dance. The studio audience applauded. The judges explained their scores. Two more dance routines and commercial breaks later, my mother finally stopped breathing.

After what felt like an excruciating amount of time, Aunty Wynn entered the room. She placed her cup of tea on the bedside table. As she reached around me to check for my mother's pulse, the stench of all of those freesias became too much, and I retched— pathetically, as if I was doing it for the attention. I felt guilty about it, for not being able to control myself.

'You okay?' Aunty Wynn said.

'Sorry,' I said, putting my hand over my mouth.

'She's gone,' she said, stepping back from the bed.

'Yes,' I said. And I felt it.

Wednesday

It had rained during the night. The neighbours' trampoline looked soaked, slick. As the kettle came to boil and I finished making my cup of tea, an old memory bubbled up of a kid goofing around on a school trampoline, the big one on the field beside the monkey bars. It had rained during the night then, too, and despite how slippery the surface was the kid was doing back flips, excited to have full reign of the trampoline, not having to share it with anyone, the other kids not wanting to get their clothes wet so early in the morning. Then, just as the kid landed another exuberant back flip, her feet shot out from underneath her, forcing her to topple and hop back towards the rusted metal springs behind her, so she ultimately landed with one leg either side of the trampoline's hard metal frame, divided in half.

Was that kid me? Or had I only witnessed the fall? I couldn't—can't—remember.

Aunty Wynn had left out for me a bag of bread, a clean plate and knife, an already hacked-at half-pound of butter, jars of honey, Marmite, marmalade, crunchy peanut butter, and three kinds of jam. I sipped my tea and I didn't know what I wanted or how to make such a basic decision. I'd heard Aunty Wynn moving around the house at different times throughout the night, and I believed she had slept as much as me, which was not at all.

'Erin,' Aunty Wynn said in a whisper.

She was standing in the doorway between the kitchen and hallway. She had been tidying my mother's bedroom—

removing the empty vial and the other instruments, smoothing my mother's duvet, so it was no longer obvious a creature had spent the night curled up at the end of the bed, all to make the room look like the scene of a natural death.

'Yes?' I asked, whispering, too, though there was no need.

'Where's the big syringe?'

'The bathroom?'

'Is that a question?'

The syringe was definitely in the bathroom. I'd put it there after I'd washed it in the bathroom basin, and used a hand towel to wipe all of the edges where I'd touched it, where I might have left my fingerprints. I'd done this without thinking about what I was doing and why.

'I washed it out,' I said. 'It's drying.'

'I usually do that in the kitchen,' Aunty Wynn said. She lingered, tried to smile, instead her nostrils flaring, eyebrows rising as she took a deep breath in.

'I'm going to call some people now,' she said.

I nodded dumbly.

'Lia made the marmalade,' she said, looking towards the selection of condiments behind me. 'It's surprisingly sweet.' She said this as if she were delivering the worst possible news, as if the marmalade had failed her like nothing else. 'Probably not your thing.'

'Probably not,' I said.

I could tell she wanted to say something else—maybe about the marmalade, maybe about a different failure. Instead, she turned and disappeared back down the hallway.

Smoothly. That was what I'd wanted—for my mother's death to go *smoothly*.

Nothing had gone wrong. It had worked. My mother had died without pain. It had happened relatively quickly. And she had been able to do at least some of it herself. Was this what

I'd meant, what I'd hoped for? All we had to do now was live with the lie: my mother went to sleep and, in the morning, we found her dead. I looked at all the openings of those jars of condiments, and I thought of the small dark hole in my mother's stomach and what it had swallowed. No, what I'd smoothly poured into it.

What I'd done.

I wasn't hungry for toast. And I could no longer look at all those jars just sitting there with their lids off—wasn't Aunty Wynn worried about ants? The lids had been left in a disorganised heap, so I started to sort through them so I could put them all away. It was while I was trying to figure out whether the crusty patches of jam on the underside of one metal lid were plum or blackcurrant that there was a knock on the door. I'd been so absorbed by my task I hadn't seen anyone walk past the kitchen window. I froze. What was someone doing coming to the house?

Aunty Wynn would know what to say to the person on the other side of the door, so I waited. Was I supposed to tell the person that my mother had died? Was I supposed to try out the lie on them, whomever they were, first? I hadn't heard Aunty Wynn on the phone yet, but maybe it was the people who would take away my mother's body? Or the police, with more questions? New questions? Or Craig? Or some unexplained person? Any person? I started to feel sick.

I willed Aunty Wynn to come my way. The fridge started to groan. Aunty Wynn didn't come. No one did.

I have since imagined Aunty Wynn standing frozen, as I was, also unable to face the person on the other side of the door. This has become the picture I see, the one I recall first, when I think of this time. Though the colours and the tones of the

199

piece have already changed, the composition never does. There I am playing statue in the dimly lit kitchen, surrounded by all of that retro furniture, the obnoxious chrome fridge, the jars of condiments gathering condensation, nervously picking at my fingernails. Standing at the far end of the hallway—somehow this all fits on the same canvas— Aunty Wynn is playing her own game of statue. She is looking in the direction of my mother's body with a phone in one hand, the family photos and books that no one will ever read filling the space behind her. Her other hand is empty. She swallows deeply while she holds her breath. I hold my breath too. And in the quiet between the knocks on the door, it is as if something resets. I feel it. I'm deeply afraid. I'm still Erin Moore. The same woman I was four days ago, one day ago. But I'm someone else now too.

Standing at the top of the kitchen steps was a small lean woman dressed in old blue jeans, a brown and green Swanndri that came down to her knees, gumboots that almost met the hem of that baggy woollen layer, and a large oilskin hat, the kind you might see on a rancher in Australia. She was swimming in those clothes.

'Who are you?' she asked. 'I haven't seen you before.'

I didn't answer. She was wearing a deep red lipstick and some expertly applied eyeliner and mascara. I could smell her perfume—a young person's fragrance.

'I was supposed to pick up the cabbages,' the woman said, her eyes lingering on the bandages on my face. 'Cliff said he'd leave them for me at the bottom of the driveway.' She sounded put out.

'The cabbages?'

'Yeah. You know where he is?' she said. 'He's not answering his door.' She adjusted her hat with one perfectly manicured

hand. The hat was scuffed and stained, and it had a plaited leather detail around its circumference that looked like the cured intestines of a small mammal.

'I couldn't say for sure,' I said carefully. 'He's probably in his garden.'

I hadn't seen Uncle Cliff since the night before, when we'd had dinner together, but I didn't want the woman to know that.

She looked over her shoulder towards Uncle Cliff's tractor-tyre gardens in the backyard, and the mostly obscured teepee ones over the fence. 'I don't see him,' she said.

I just stared at her. I was no longer trying to figure out whether I should tell her my mother had just died—I was trying to figure out *how* to tell her. How to say the words. They weren't on the tip of my tongue, they were in the back of my throat. Firmly lodged.

'Never mind,' the woman said, resigned, as if she were too used to being let down to be bothered by it anymore. 'I'll get the cabbages myself.'

I shivered. The cold air from outside was spinning its way past my legs. I hadn't realised how warm it was inside the kitchen till then.

'Do you need anything?' I asked.

'Nope.' She dug into one of the pockets of her Swanndri and pulled out a bone-handled folding-knife—all smooth edges, well-worn and loved—and a fistful of used plastic shopping bags. 'I just didn't want you to think I'm some kind of thief.'

Before I could muster a response, the woman was marching across the backyard. I watched as she squatted at the edge of one of Uncle Cliff's gardens, and with a forceful swipe of her knife freed one cabbage of its root. She took out another, and another, rolling each of the cabbages into the plastic shopping bags. I couldn't watch her any longer, so I closed the door.

The kitchen was freezing now—all that chilled morning air

from outside was inside. I blew on my hands and slid them into my jeans pockets. I didn't know what to do. About the cold, or anything else. My mother would have taken a dislike to the woman with the knife, I thought. On imagining her joyful disdain I felt a small comfort, which was immediately followed by something new. Something immense, heavy, slow-moving, loud. I could hear birds frantically cheeping in a shrub beneath the kitchen window. And then I heard Aunty Wynn on the phone. She was explaining to the person on the other end in a clear, firm voice, a voice that I could hold on to, that her sister had died, and now this was what we needed.

BOOK CLUB QUESTIONS

The Swimmers is set in Chloe Lane's homeland of New Zealand. Did you feel that the novel had a strong sense of place? Or did its universal themes of family and mortality make it feel it could be set anywhere?

Do you think that Erin's reaction on first hearing the news of her mother's decision is believable? Why do you think that Erin reacts the way that she does?

Do you think Erin is a sympathetic character?

How do you feel the relationships between the main characters in *The Swimmers* contrast with other literary portrayals of female relationships and family dynamics?

The novel's heavy themes are contrasted with moments of humour and blackly comic scenes. What was your experience reading a novel with this kind of contrast?

Erin never quite comes to a conclusion about why she steals the painting from Craig's house, though she muses on the possible reasons while in the police station. Why do you think Erin stole the painting?

How did you feel about the end of the novel, was it what you expected?

The Swimmers is divided into parts specifying the days leading up to Erin's mother's death. Why do you think this was done? What effect does it create?

Though *The Swimmers* is focused on its female characters, several

male characters impact the narrative: Karl, Craig, Uncle Cliff and Stephen the vet. Do you think the novel makes any statements about relationships between men and women?

Is *The Swimmers* an uplifting novel?

Q and A with Chloe Lane, February 2022

How long have you been writing? Why did you start?
I started writing when I was in art school in the early 2000s. My publications from that time were mostly reviews and profiles of exhibitions or other artists. Looking back, the shift I made from that kind of writing to fiction wasn't a huge stretch, as many of the things I wrote then included unnecessary fictional elements like detailed character descriptions and dialogue. Around 2005 I published a short profile on an artist who is now based in Berlin. I can't remember exactly what I said or if I even pulled it off, but I do recall the feeling of how much fun it was to write, how much the page felt like the place I should be. It took me a while longer to completely let go of wanting an art career, to put down that instrument, but I have those years to thank for introducing me to writing, this other instrument, which I have learned to play better.

What were your favourite books growing up?
I was fortunate to grow up in a house full of books. I read all the fiction on our shelves, including books my parents had from their youths, and what I picked up on fortnightly trips to the library. For my tenth birthday my parents bought me the complete *The Lord of the Rings* in one huge, illustrated, hardback volume. I lugged that tome in its own plastic bag to school and back every day, so I might have it on hand for SSR (sustained silent reading). There were probably more books of non-fiction on our shelves than fiction, in particular on art and architecture, as well as a collection of volumes from the 1970s about the supernatural, and many *National Geographics*. All of these I loved. Having said that, the books I remember most vividly from my earlier reading years were adventure stories. Though decades have passed since I cracked one of those novels, I can recall scenes from those pages as vividly as if they were things that I experienced in the flesh.

What inspired you to write *The Swimmers*?

I was curious to see what it might look like for a regular New Zealand family to help take the life of one of their own. I was interested in the emotional story—the toll this takes on each family member, and how they deal with their grief, guilt and obligations to the ones they love. But the logistics of carrying out an assisted suicide in a country where it is illegal, at least during the time the novel was set, that's what drives the story forward. For me the death and its means is the necessary awful thing in *The Swimmers* that allows the reader to see more deeply what Erin and Aunty Wynn are made of.

The Swimmers is set in your native New Zealand, but the bulk of the novel was written in Florida. Do you think that affected the process of writing it at all?

During the years I worked on the book, my husband and I house sat for a friend a lot during the summer months. The windows in her writing room overlooked a lake in North Central Florida, so while I was trying to write about the rural north of New Zealand with its gorse-pocked paddocks, manuka woods and subdivisions of kitset homes, I could see alligators doing laps in the water. More than once I looked out and saw a turtle digging a nest in the sandy earth above the lake's edge, depositing her eggs, and then hurrying back to the water. I also saw raccoons, possums, armadillos, snakes, all kinds of water birds, and unbelievable lightning storms from that room. None of these things make me think of New Zealand. I started writing *The Swimmers* my first summer in Florida though, so we'd been living there only about a year. When everything I was learning about writing was also starting to click in new ways—I was initially in Florida studying towards an MFA at the University of Florida—I found it helpful to have a place I could write about that I felt comfortable with, a solid foundation. I guess New Zealand will always be that place for me.

Erin is a former competitive swimmer and an art lover, are either of these elements drawn from your own experiences?

I was a competitive swimmer as a teenager. Swimming was my first true love, and those years of intense training and competition continue to make an impact on my life. Though I trained with a squad, swimming is quite a lonely sport, all those hours with your head in the water, pacing up and down. I think being drawn to that life prepared me for the writing life, which can also be a little lonely. Erin is wired in a similar way. She is determined to carve out her own path, everyone else be damned, though it's a character trait that softens in her by the end of the novel. Like Erin, I also didn't make it as an artist, though art, specifically painting, was my second love. One of my favourite New Zealand painters, Nicola Farquhar, provided the painting, titled "Peachthief," for the cover image in both the Gallic Books and New Zealand releases of *The Swimmers*.

The novel contrasts a difficult subject matter with a lot of sardonic humour and eccentric scenes. Was this an intentional style or did it come about organically?

Whenever I try to be funny I am not funny, so any laughs I get are generally unintentional. Though maybe that isn't entirely accurate. I think what I do try for is the kind of realism that acknowledges that some of the heaviest, darkest moments of our lives, can also be woven through with unexpected levity. Or failing that, an absurdness that is inescapable because life is absurd.

What are you currently reading?

I have just started reading the new Claire Vaye Watkins novel, *I Love You But I've Chosen Darkness*. I adored her first story collection, *Battleborn*, and so far this one is even funnier and more brutal. I regularly teach one of her short stories in my fiction classes as an example of how to write about place in such

a way that it rises up to occupy the space of another character. The story, titled "Man-O-War," is set in the desert, and you can practically feel the heat and the dust rising up from the pages.

Are there any books or authors you reread and return to?
This is one of the joys of teaching fiction for me—the cache of authors I will always teach and so be forced to re-read on a regular basis. Anton Chekhov, William Trevor, and Joy Williams are three I enjoy revisiting in my role as a teacher.

What does your writing routine look like?
My dream writing routine is to be up early and write till lunch, and then take the afternoon to do other things: paid work, exercise, read. Of course this isn't always possible, and since my son was born (he's now three years old), I've gotten better at switching in and out of writing mode, and making the most of whatever time is available. The only time I don't like to write is at night, as I am a terrible sleeper, and if I don't put enough hours between imaginative work and bedtime, I will not sleep at all.

What are you working on right now?
I have nearly finished writing my second novel. It is titled *Arms & Legs*, and it tells the story of Georgie, a New Zealand woman in her thirties living in a small University town in North Central Florida, and what happens when she discovers the remains of a missing student while volunteering on a prescribed burn. The novel details how finding the boy's body shakes her and seeps into the many cracks in her life, resulting in acts of violence both physical and emotional. It's also a bit of a love letter to Florida.